AN EXTREME LOVE STORY

BY

CHRISTOPHER ROBERTSON

D & T
PUBLISHING

Warning:
Don't read unless you're cool with some very kinky,
VERY fucked up shit.

Nasty, icky, filthy, and sticky!
Fuck it, I love it!
Dirty, creepy, thirsty, and freaky!
Fuck it, I love it!

Lil Mariko (Disgusting)

What the fuck is wrong with you? Why are you reading this?

You know there's some really fucked up, kinky, and gross shit in here, right?

You're cool with that… well, shit, here's the soundtrack you sick fuck.

Or search for Babydoll on Spotify.

https://open.spotify.com/playlist/71nTSsomD0AAk0Y0rou5eg?si=2R2sBWQYQzq4u1UFdDKGKw&utm_source=copy-link

For all you fuckin' perverts.

BABYDOLL

"So, that happened...," says a guy with puppy dog eyes, a bloodied nose, and a busted lip.

"Yup," says a girl with runny mascara, frazzled rainbow hair, balancing precariously on shoes missing a heel.

The two of them stand in the midday sun, the occasional car passing through the industrial park behind them, as they stare along a polluted river. Rusted trolley carts break the surface like urban coral. Slowly, they turn to look one another in the eye. He sighs, she gulps, and –

Twenty - Four Hours
A g o ...

"Is it just yourself staying with us this evening, Mr. Barton?"

C h e c k - I n .

The guy the check-in girl's talking to doesn't answer. He's too busy looking around a hotel lobby that doesn't want to be one. Like, there's no check-in desk, and she's in black jeans, matching button-down shirt, and

Chuck Taylors with a tablet strapped to one hand. Cool, purple hair sweeps back from pretty, round eyes and lashes made for fluttering. Disney Dalmatian earrings dangle from her ears, and her badge says her name's Alana.

"Mr. Barton?"

"Oh, hey, sorry," the guy rubs the back of his neck in embarrassment. His laugh is honest, infectious, and the way his effortless floppy hair bounces makes her smile. "This place is really cool!"

He keeps looking at a giant TV wedged into a ten-foot-tall bookcase playing a loop of Kaijus going at it. Gigan's currently fucking up Rodan to a cute J-Pop beat. Two currently unoccupied heart-shaped love-seat-sofas face it with a color-changing coffee table between them.

"Yeah, it's an XOX thing," Alana explains, tapping the logo pin on her shirt – an anime cat head with two Xs for eyes and a gaping O mouth.

"Huh?"

"XOX, the *Hentai Hotel*…"

"Woah, like with tentacles and stuff?"

She stares at him like he just farted in an elevator. "More like a cool place for adults to hang out and have fun than a hotel. The bar over there's open twenty-four-seven, and there are Japanese-style vending machines on every floor."

"The ones with panties?"

"No... for coffee and snacks..."

"Ah," the guy smiles so wide his eyes almost vanish, "gotcha."

"Um, so is it just yourself?" she asks again, thinking she wouldn't mind giving him a pair of her panties if that's what he wants — or shoving them in his mouth.

"What? Oh, no, my girlfriend's coming, too. She's just got, like, some work stuff. I said I'd check us in so she can just relax."

"Aw, how sweet," of course. Alana's lip twitches. She taps away on her tablet, maybe a little too hard. "Just one key, then?"

"Better make it two," the guy says and checks out a revolving sushi bar serving artisanal cupcakes shaped like tentacles and uwu ahegao faces. "She's having a girl's night, you know?"

That confuses Alana. "So, you're not staying?"

"Oh, yeah, I am. I'll just chill here till she gets back. Do you have those movies in the rooms?" He nods to the TV. "I wanna see who wins." He winces as Rodan takes a whack.

"Sure, we have hundreds of Japanese cult movies and anime on demand," Alana hits the button to verify and loads two keycards into the readers on her podium, and a thought occurs. A naughty one. "So, I get off at ten." She hands him the cards, making sure to graze his fingers with hers. "If you're lonely sitting around waiting for your girlfriend, we could get a drink at the bar? I can even tell you who wins."

"Cool!" He takes the cards. "Awesome, thanks,"

and completely ignores her offer.

As the clueless, cute goofball heads to the elevator, Alana calls after him, "Have a fun night!"

He gives her a thumbs up and a wave before disappearing into the elevator.

The door opens again on the third floor, onto a three-way intersection. He follows an arrow to the left, walking along a wall covered in Japanese graffiti behind color-changing glass till he gets to the right door.

A swipe of his card and the door opens all on its own, silently.

"Woah, this place is awesome!" He steps past curved, exposed built-in storage shelves to the right with a wall of frosted glass on the left. A seamless sliding door towards a massive bed dominates half the room, flush to both sides, and the wall-spanning picture window at the far-side. There's a wallpaper-thin TV mounted at one end of the bed against shiny black brickwork, with the hotel's anime kitty logo winking an X-shaped eye every couple of seconds on screen.

Picking up a tablet from a beside half-table, he starts hitting options, trying to figure out how to get the TV on. Behind him, the frosted glass changes hues, from red to blue to purple and back. The roller blinds go down on their own.

"This is nuts!" He's like a kid with a brand new video-game console. "Oh, there!" He flicks something on the tablet, and suddenly, the Toho Co., Ltd. logo appears on the TV.

Kicking his boots off, he hops up on the bed, lies back, pumped to see the fight, and kicks back.

Down in the lobby, a girl barely five feet despite black heels she wears below skin-tight faux leather leggings and a baggy, half-tucked in white shirt, clacks across the tiles. She pushes a suitcase two-thirds her size beside her. Hair pinned up inside a saggy black beret, eyes hidden behind impenetrable Ray-Bans.

She struts through the lobby like she belongs, like she's been there before, and heads straight towards the elevators, ignoring the check-in podiums. Passing the loveseats, she smirks as she spots a middle-aged woman, shoes off, feet up, reading a copy of Princess Bubblegum and The Slumber Party War–the neon pinks and purples of the cover contrasting beautifully with her business chic.

She approaches the lift and reaches out, but there's no button—just a keycard sensor. "Dammit—"

"Can I help?" Alana skips over, doing a slight head turn.

"Yeah, I'm supposed to meet my boyfriend, hang on," she takes out a phone, unlocks it with her finger, and checks the latest texts. "We're in room…"

"It's cool," Alana smiles and holds her badge to the reader. "Have a fun stay with XOX!"

"Thank you," the other woman says, then as the door closes, "that's the plan." She and her massive case ride the elevator decorated with an oversized black and white art photo of two anime women kissing.

She makes it to the room and knocks on the door. While she waits, she looks up and down the corridor; there's no sign of anyone, so she whips the beret off – rainbow-colored hair tumbles free.

The door opens, and she looks over the rim of her shades at a goofy smile and fully erect cock poking out below a beige hoodie.

"Oh, you're a naughty boy. Who said you can start without me?" She goes on her tiptoes, kisses him, slaps his dick, and then pushes past, wheeling her case into the room.

P r e p

"Are you gonna sit there and watch? Or do you wanna make yourself useful?" The woman kneeling by the mirror, surrounded by a half-dozen open makeup palettes and a smoking curling iron asks. Naked, rainbow-colored hair pinned flat to her scalp, she flits between palettes with automatic expertise and still has enough concentration to watch the TV in the mirror and throw a glare at the guy on the bed.

"You know I love watchin' you get ready," he says, casually jacking it with one hand, smiling and winking at her with that golden retriever energy. He genuinely loves seeing her prepare for playtime; it's like spying on a present getting wrapped, like watching the sprinkles rain down on your ice cream. God, he wants to lick her ass so much right now. Speaking of eating, "You meeting the girls for dinner first? Wanna order in?"

"You know I hate eating before playing." Wafts of steam rise as she runs curlers through the wig.

"God, I love it when you say shit like that." He does; it's easy to see how hard that makes him though she pretends not to notice. "What name are you playing with tonight? In case, you know?"

"Sara?"

"No, you used that before. Gotta keep it anonymous, Babydoll."

"What's the porn star we watched last night called?"

"The redhead? Maitland Ward?"

"No, Honeybear, the other one," Babydoll holds the curler between her teeth as she puts the wig on, hiding her distinctive hair and suddenly looking a hell of a lot more sultry.

Honeybear groans.

"The one you said looked just like me? And you were all," she puts on a silly and oddly sexy pretend male voice, " *'God, it's like watching you get fucked by a porn star, oh Babydoll, please do that one day? You'd look so hot getting drilled on deeper.com. Hashtag couple goals.'*"

"Tell me I'm wrong," Honeybear insists.

Babydoll bites her lip at the thought, "If only. Anyway, what's her name?"

"Lulu Chu."

"Wow, you didn't even have to look it up," Babydoll giggles.

"I've got a good memory!"

"Sure," Babydoll threatens him with the curler, "have you been naughty, Honeybear? You know no touchy-touchy before playtime."

"Noooooo," he looks away. "Okay maybe a little, but only because when she's getting it from behind, I can pretend it's you! God, I wish you'd let me watch! Or make a video for me?"

"Hmm," Babydoll glares, her slight features scrunching, "no." And she turns back to the mirror. "Lulu," she gives that name a test. "Hi. I'm Lulu, wanna come back to my room and fuck?"

"I mean, you got me hard," Honeybear jokes and wags a lap rocket ready for launch.

"You're always hard," Babydoll rolls her eyes.

"That's 'cause you're always so fucking hot," he leaps off the bed and goes to her, crouching down to cup her breasts from behind. "You know, if you let me hide in the room, I promise to be quiet."

"Nope, Honeyboo, you know the rules, and don't mess up my hair!"

"God, I love it when you're a bitch. Spit in my mouth and call me trash?"

"No," Babydoll resumes her routine, "you'd like it too much. Now go sit down and watch your girlfriend get prettied up to go fuck some stranger."

"Yes, ma'am!" He salutes and puts himself down in the chair.

The way he does as he's told, like a good little puppy, gives Babydoll a twinge in her heart, and she cuts him some slack. "Maybe, if you're good, later. After someone cums in my mouth."

"Please do not threaten me with a good time."

"What name are you using, Honeybear?" Babydoll asks. "Just in case."

"Clint."

"Are you serious?"

"What?"

"Nobody's called Clint!"

"Clint Eastwood! Clint Barton!"

"Who's the second one?"

"Hawkeye?"

"Who?"

"Avenger. Bow and arrow dude."

"Oh, the one Avenger nobody wants to fuck, good idea." Babydoll clicks her curling iron off and stands up, fanning herself with her hands.

"I know you're not dissing my guy, Hawkeye."

"All I'm saying is if I was getting gangbanged by the Avenger's…"

"What?"

"Nothing. Just had an idea. Anyway, surprised you didn't pick a name to fit the hotel. We could have done Chainsawman?"

"Yeah, well, you can pass for Makima, but I don't exactly look like a Denji."

"True," Babydoll smirks. "But you're just as good a doggy, aren't you?"

Honeybear brings his hands to his chin and pants like a happy pup. She laughs – her Honeybear might be a complete moron, but he's an entertaining one. Not to mention cute.

"Still got time," Babydoll eyes her tight black leather dress, laid out on the chair. "Not like we can go to the bar for a drink, can't be seen together and all that. So..."

"So..." Honeybear hops off the bed and comes up behind her. "Wanna fuck?"

"Yeah, but not with you," Babydoll sticks her tongue out.

"Bitch," Honeybear growls. "I love it."

"Help me with my shoes," Babydoll perches on the edge of the bed, crossing her legs and pointing the pedicured toes of one foot at Honeybear.

He drops to his knees like nothing could make him happier and reaches for her red stilettos. His eyes never leave Babydoll. They gaze up along her leg, meeting hers as she stares down at him, smirking.

Babydoll strokes Honeybear's lips with her toe, and she feels them part in response. What the hell? He's been such a good boy, booking her this room, surprising her with these new heels this morning. She can't wait to get fucked in them.

Honeybear opens his mouth, and Babydoll slides her toe in – she feels his tongue lick her instantly; it tickles in all the right ways. His mouth opens wider, so she pushes more of her foot in, enough to fill his whole mouth. Enough to shove his head back, make him choke. Maybe later, she'll let him lick some guy's cum off her pretty, painted toes.

"God damn," Honeybear gasps, strings of saliva linking his gaping mouth with Babydoll's foot. He tries to catch his breath, and Babydoll coughs for attention. "Oh, sorry," Honeybear apologizes and dries her foot off with the bottom of his hoodie. "That's so cute," he says, noticing the five different neon colors, a different one on each toe.

"You like?" Babydoll lines her toes up, wiggles them, "Zack squeezed me in even though he's fully booked."

"Yeah, that's 'cause he wants another blowjob," Honeybear wipes the spit from his chin.

"You said you weren't mad!" Babydoll gasps.

"I wasn't! But you know we can't play with anyone who knows us. If we get caught…"

"I know," Babydoll sulks, "I know. Shoes, now, Honeyboo."

"Sorry, miss," Honeybear takes one of the red heels and slides it lovingly onto Babydoll's extended foot. He holds it gently in place and fixes the buckle, grazing her delicate ankle. Babydoll switches legs, giving her boyfriend a quick glimpse between them. It's enough to see she's fully waxed. She doesn't need to say anything; Babydoll knows her Honeybear will get the implication. That he'll know it won't look so pristine next time he sees it.

"God, I wanna eat you so much right now," he says like he's testing the water, vaguely posturing if that could be a possibility.

"I hope you're not asking," Babydoll scowls. "You know you're not allowed."

"I know," Honeybear sulks. His eyebrow spikes, "but we didn't say anything about your ass? Did we?"

Babydoll bites her lip, thinks it over, and can't find any pre-established reason to deny him. "I suppose, but just there, you hear me?"

"Yes, miss!" Honeybear salutes as he salivates at the thought.

"But you have to do it while I do my lipstick; it's getting late," Babydoll slides off the bed and walks to the mirror in nothing but her heels. She arches her back, half-turns to check out how she looks – shiny nipple piercings more prominent than her itty-bitty titties.

Honeybear follows on his knees as Babydoll rummages for her lipstick. She leans over, pouting her butt as she purses her lips in the mirror. As the lipstick touches down, so does Honeybear's tongue. Her tiny tushie isn't hard for him to get his tongue through, and his nose nuzzles the top of her crack. Babydoll nearly loses focus, smearing her lipstick, as her Honeybear's tongue pushes through any resistance, curling inside her delicate little hole.

Honeybear moans like it's the tastiest treat of all time and pulls her cheeks apart with his hands to get deeper inside his Babydoll's ass.

It takes all her focus to keep applying the lipstick. She's not about to let Honeybear know she loves what he's doing. Not that he needs the encouragement, Honeybear always eats her like it's his birthday and she's his cake.

"I better not feel that tongue anyway near anything else," Babydoll warns as she finishes with her lips. She blows a kiss, lets her Honeybear nuzzle on her booty for a little bit more, then says, "That's enough," as she reaches around and slaps his cheek.

Honeybear falls back with a soft pop, gasping with delight. He looks up at his slutty goddess in awe. "Thank you, miss, that was delicious."

"Well, duh," Babydoll says all Billie Eilish-style. She nudges him with her shoe. "Get my underwear for me."

Honeybear does as he's told, fishing a dark red thong and matching lace bralette from Babydoll's overnight bag. She doesn't need the bra; it's more for window dressing.

"May I?" Honeybear asks, holding the thong for her.

Babydoll nods and steps into it, allowing her Honeybear to slide them up along her smooth, olive thighs, pulling it till the string almost disappears.

He gets the bralette next and Babydoll faces the mirror, holding her arms up for her Honeybear to slip it over her arms. As he fastens the clasps, he notices they're cutaways, the wire curving under her tiny tits, more putting them on display than offering support.

"Woah," Honeybear says, and he admires her in the mirror. He rests his chin on her shoulder and wraps his arms around her waist. "You look gorgeous... Lulu."

"Thank you," Babydoll smiles and then rolls her eyes, "Clint."

"You know I love it when you get new lingerie for playtime, somethin' about you getting fucked by someone else in it for the first time just does it for me."

Babydoll giggles. "Who says I haven't been fucked in this before?"

"God! Damn! I could kiss you!"

Honeybear leans in to do so, and Babydoll shoves him away.

"Eww, no, not after where your mouth's just been," she puts her hands on her hips and nods to the rest of her outfit. "Now help me with my dress, or I'm gonna be late."

Honeybear does that, and as he zips her up, the thought that someone else will be pulling the same zip down later that evening sends his stomach into delicious turmoil.

"I'll call an Uber," Honeybear says as Babydoll checks how she looks.

Many little moments act like thresholds for Honeybear, but one of the final ones that says this is absolutely happening, that his Babydoll's going out to play and he can't stop her, is when the Uber app says driver assigned. It's the way the ETA acts like a countdown that does it for him. In seven minutes, her ride will be here, ready to carry her beyond his reach, into the night and God knows what trouble.

"Seven minutes till Heaven, Babydoll," he jokes and then watches as she checks out how she looks from behind. Damn good, he wants to say, but instead takes a moment to quietly stroke his cock while his girlfriend doesn't even notice him.

Or, at least, that's what he thinks.

"Um, what are you doing?"

"Come on; you can't look that good and expect me not to. Do you remember when you used to tell me to cum over you before you went out with the girls?"

"Maybe?"

"Said it gave you confidence?"

"Hmm… nope, Honeyboo, you know the rules."

"Aww, please?"

"No! Now be a good boy and tell me when you're allowed to cum."

"After you've gotten your pussy filled up by some random stranger," Honeybear groans.

"And..."

"And after I lick up all the honey," he smiles.

"That's a good boy," she pats his face. "You can stay in the room till I need it," she glances around, "but clean up for me."

Babydoll picks up her handbag on the way to the door and checks she has what she needs: keycard, bank card, fake ID... condoms.

"Really?" Back in the early days, finding condoms in her purse meant she had permission to play, but she's way past asking for approval these days. Babydoll throws Honeybear a disapproving stare then drops them in the bin. Her bear needs his honey, after all.

"I love you, Babydoll," Honeybear says as he sees her off at the door.

"I love you too, Honeybear," she says and blows him a kiss, then leaves him, mind racing, about all the debauched possibilities that lie ahead.

Play Time

Honeybear struts past the mirror, full-on Winnie the Pooh, top on pants off, except that particular honey bear didn't rock a massive hard-on. At least, it was never confirmed. Tigger did always bounce like he was keeping his ass off the ground, though. Almost like it hurts…

He stops to check himself out, striking a pose before flopping on the bed.

One arm behind his head, the other unlocking his phone as he unwinds and tries not to think of his girlfriend currently in an Uber. In that dress. And those heels. Honeybear knows he's not allowed to jack off yet, but Babydoll never said anything about shaking it around, maybe slapping it a little...

His hand grips the base of his dick just as his phone buzzes.

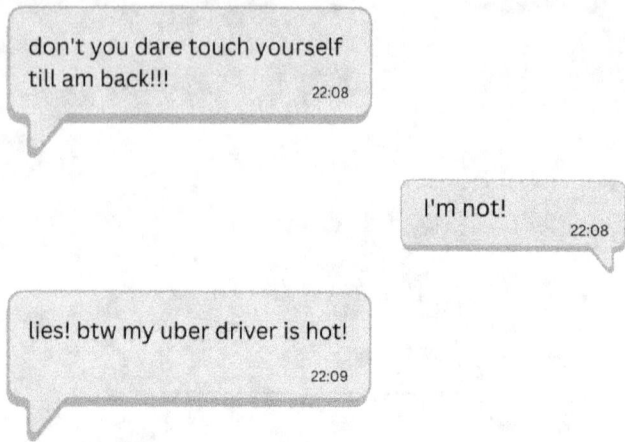

don't you dare touch yourself
till am back!!!
22:08

I'm not!
22:08

lies! btw my uber driver is hot!
22:09

Honeybear groans. Babydoll knows damn well her Honeybear has a fantasy about her fucking an Uber driver. Getting all dressed up, going for the ride, and then making out her plans got canceled. She'd act all sad, like her night's wasted, and wait for him to offer to take her out. She'd suggest just finding somewhere private to pull over.

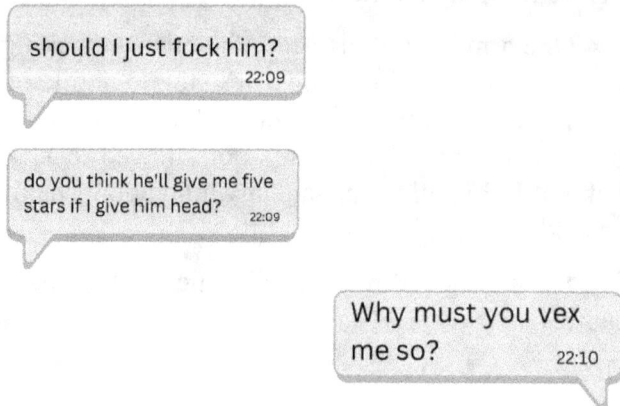

should I just fuck him?
22:09

do you think he'll give me five
stars if I give him head?
22:09

Why must you vex
me so?
22:10

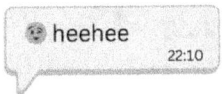

heehee
22:10

He drops his phone on his chest, grumbling something about an evil, demented kink pixie. The phone buzzes again, vibrating his ribcage and snapping him away from perverse thoughts about his girlfriend's face and palms flat against steamy windows in some empty parking lot.

at the club. he gave me his number if "I need a lift" 😏
22:23

That makes Honeybear smile and nod; maybe she's not just teasing after all.

ok GTG if I don't respond it's cause I'm sucking D! Love youuuu! 😘
22:24

He looks at the time, it's only just after ten, and there's little to no chance his Babydoll will be coming back this side of midnight. The boredom is part of it; the long periods of radio silence from his Babydoll only add to the sweet torment, but he best keep busy.

Still in nothing but his t-shirt, Honeybear sets about tidying up the room. He puts Babydoll's things away carefully, enjoying the scent of her perfume. The one she only wears when she plays.

He packs all her stuff away in her soft pink hard-shell-wheeled suitcase that he knows for a fact is almost half the size of his Babydoll. While he's at it, Honeybear puts his stuff away, too, making sure there's no trace of him in the room except for his pants, underwear, and shoes that he'll throw on when he needs to.

The next hour he spends checking his phone every couple of seconds, trying to focus on a movie and not think about his naughty ass girlfriend slutty dancing with random guys. Hands taking sneaky feels of the ass he was tongue deep in just a short while ago.

If he knew what club, he could pop along. Lurk in the dark, watch his Babydoll work. Hands splayed on some guy's chest, throwing her hair back as she shakes her booty. Wiggling her way down her body, hands going to the guy's belt. Bodies packed around them, sweaty, a pounding beat, his belt comes free, and Babydoll teases his zip-

BUZZ!

If there's one thing his Babydoll can not be reproached on, it's her timing.

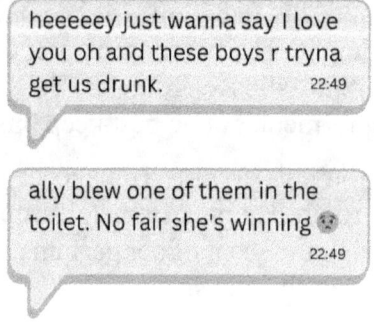

heeeeey just wanna say I love you oh and these boys r tryna get us drunk.   22:49

ally blew one of them in the toilet. No fair she's winning 💀   22:49

Honeybear shakes his head.

It's not a race, BabyD. 22:50

yes it is and she's winning! fuckin slut! and he's a rugby player! no fair! 22:51

I'll show her 😈 22:51

Half an hour later, his phone buzzes again.

hehehe got one 23:12

Honeybear's heart skips a beat at reading those two simple words. There's always a chance she goes out and doesn't find a suitable playmate. She's fussy, after all, and despite already racking up an impressive body count, not just anyone will do. She needs both a physical and mental attraction, meaning sometimes it doesn't happen, and all that build up is for nothing. Not that he doesn't enjoy regular sex with his sweet Babydoll. They do that often enough, that's not it - it's just some bottles you can't cork once they're popped. Some couples have a list of celebrities they're allowed to hook-up with, on the off chance. Others shop for monster dildos on Etsy together. It's basically the same.

> Details please?
> 23:12

> tall, blue eyes, awesome
> kisser. freakin hawt swimmer's
> body.
> 23:14

A photo follows seconds later, Babydoll leaning against a slender, lean yet muscular man, her head thrown back in an open-mouthed laugh as he poses like he's cool, but he's just drunk. She barely reaches halfway up his chest. Honeybear's got to admit; he's a handsome guy. Steely eyes, a light dusting of stubble, thick, shiny dirty blonde hair barely held back in chunky waves. His Babydoll done good.

> oh and his name is
> Clint!!!
> 23:14

"Of course!" Honeybear says to the empty hotel room.

> you know the rules Honeyboo.
> stop playing with yourself and
> get the room ready.
> 23:17

As comfortable as he is, Honeybear has no objections to that. He fights his hard on, forcing it down as he pulls his pants back on, then slips into his shoes. One quick check of the room to make sure everything's out of the way, then he heads down to the bar.

"Yo, can I get a…" Honeybear squints at the digital cocktail menu. An anime character accompanies every drink; from the looks of it, he wouldn't survive one sip of a Detroit Smasher. "A Sharingan Spinner?"

TVs above the bar show a looping reel of Dragonball's best fights. With the crackly Lofi Japanese chill-hop layered over it and an abundance of shirtless, muscular, grunting Goku on Vegeta action, the show suddenly seems more homoerotic than Honeybear recalls. Also, there's a purple cat person now. He's so transfixed by it he doesn't notice the bartender present him with a dark red drink with black swirls on the surface.

The place is pretty empty, so he has no trouble picking the right spot. Somewhere he can watch the door and the elevator without making it look suspicious. He settles in, sipping his drink, and waits. God, the waiting is delicious. It shouldn't be long; it's too cold to walk, and in those heels, not to mention how horny she'll be, they'll have jumped a cab. His hands will be on her naked thigh, moving up her dress. She'll be pulling him in, making him kiss her neck.

"Hey there," a kinda familiar voice interrupts Honeybear's perverted fantasies.

Honeybear looks up to see the check-in girl, Alana, sans name badge and the top buttons on her shirt now open. She motions to the seat across from him, and, just to be polite, Honeybear nods for her to sit.

"You look as bored as I feel."

Honeybear flashes an honest smile, "I'm cool, my girl's got a night on the town with her friends, so I got us a room."

"Yeah, I know," Alana feels a little upset by that, "I checked you in."

"Oh, sorry, my bad," Honeybear apologies. "I didn't recognize you without your name tag."

Ok, that hurts.

"So, what, are you just waiting for her? Like a puppy?"

Suddenly he imagines himself wearing a dog collar, Babydoll holding the lead as she struts around some fetish club in nothing but thigh-high latex stockings. She chains him up outside the door, and he sits there like a good boy while she enters a dark room where several naked, shadowy forms wait.

"Eh, clubs aren't really my scene," Honeybear shrugs. *The normal kind anyway.* "Besides, she needs some girl time, you know?"

Alana sips her drink, "That's cute. In a simp kinda way."

"Really?"

"Yeah, like, no offense, but she could be out there grinding on some guy right now, and here you are just waiting for her."

If only, Honeybear almost says, "I trust her."

"That's sweet." She takes another drink, "I wouldn't."

"That so?"

"Yeah, and you know what," Alana leans in, her leg brushes Honeybear's. He doesn't pull away, nor does he respond. "I think you should teach her a lesson?"

"Sorry," Honeybear says; he can smell that this isn't her first drink of the evening. "You're beautiful and all that, but I'm not that guy."

"Really?" She leans in, letting Honeybear see down her shirt. He notices but doesn't stare. "What if you knew for a fact that she was getting deep dicked right now?" Alana smirks and raises her eyebrows, daring him to answer.

He doesn't let it show on his face, but Honeybear loves the way that it hits his ear. "Even so," he says with absolute certainty.

"Wow," she enunciates each syllable dramatically. "Why are the pretty ones so dumb," she strokes Honeybear's cheek and then downs the rest of her drink. Calling it a loss, she stands up to leave as Babydoll and her date stumbles into the lobby, laughing like they don't care if anyone stares. The guy who looks like Chris Hemsworth and Ryan Gosling did a fusion dance with his arm around her shoulder. Hers crosses his back and can only reach toward his neck thanks to the heels.

"Looks like they're having fun at least."

"Here's hoping," Honeybear says under his breath and takes a sip of his drink.

No matter how many times they've done this, moments like this always fill him with an uneasy cocktail of anxiety and excitement. The sight of another man, holding his girlfriend, unaware she's taken, that the man she loves is watching them pass. The way she places hers on him, boldly unashamed. It doesn't sit easy in his gut; it's not supposed to, and if it did, this wouldn't be any fun.

They cross the lobby together, the click of heels on tiles and teasing giggles echoing. It's genuine, but also for show. One thing that always excites Honeybear is how much his Babydoll gives herself to her playmates; it's why she insists on playing alone. And because it drives her Honeybear wild.

Babydoll knows better than to look at her Honeybear, and they pass within inches, like total strangers. He can smell that perfume again, that scent of delicious debasement. It triggers a Pavlovian response, immediately making him picture Babydoll's lithe little body all sweaty, legs wide apart as some faceless muscular back thrusts into her. Perfectly manicured fingernails digging into the skin, begging him to go deeper. Forgetting all about her Honeybear at that moment, her whole world just intense pleasure.

God, he loves that. The conflict, the way jealousy bubbles with admiration, sets him at tantalizing unease. He rides that disquiet, reveling in the powerlessness, something rare and precious to him. No other man gets to enjoy this side of her.

Babydoll and her date slip into the elevator. She pins him to the wall, forcefully, the sound loud enough to draw stares. She's making sure her Honeybear's watching, as though he'd want to look anywhere else. She kicks one heel up and leans back, inviting the stranger to kiss her. He does, copping a feel, and Honeybear's stomach turns as he watches. He can't escape the thought he knows that guy, though. He looks familiar. His Babydoll has a type, sure, and most of them look similar, but still, he can't help but think he knows this one.

Honeybear takes another sip. They'll be in the room soon. Kissing. His hands will be fumbling with the zip at the back of her dress. She will be tugging at his belt. They'll be kissing so much, so passionately they'll not be able to focus – the desire to fuck so strong it gets in the way.

Sometimes, he's amazed at how far they've come. When they first started these games, they had rules. Like no kissing. Too romantic. He said no, she did it anyway and now the very thought puts him at risk of blowing his load.

Honeybear takes another sip of fancy drink and it hits hard, like freezing him in a single moment. And, in the moment, he sees Babydoll in her underwear now, and the lucky guy will be staring, unsure what to be blown away by - the peephole bralette presenting her small, hard nipples or the glinting metal of the piercings cutting through them. He sees her on the edge of the bed, in nothing but his shorts, as she drops to her knees and teases his cock out, licking up and down him like it's a lollipop then resting the fully hard thing against her face. He sees him grab that perfectly curled hair that Honeybear wasn't allowed to mess up and make her swallow the whole thing. Not that she'll put up a fight.

Honeybear takes one more sip and sees, in his mind, the stranger inside her now. Without a condom. Another former rule. But as Babydoll said the first time she made him lick another man's honey from her sugar cookie, rules are made to be broken. There's nothing like the thrill of crossing a once forbidden line, after all.

He's lost in thoughts of cum dribbling down his Babydoll's lips; her tongue held out with a milky pool of it quivering before she pulls it in, closing her mouth – only opening it again to show him it's all gone. He thinks about kissing her at that exact moment when his phone buzzes. It buzzes again and again as he fumbles in his pocket for it.

help!!!
23:51

I fucked up!!!
23:51

hurry!!!
23:51

His phone buzzes again and again, but neither that nor Honeybear's rocking makes the elevator go any faster.

"Fuck, move it," he growls. They're not even on the top floor, "the hell's taking so long."

The fear that their games could go wrong is never far from Honeybear's thoughts, and as much as he trusts her, knows his Babydoll can look after herself, she makes herself very vulnerable when she plays. Especially with her preference for tall, strong men who can pick her up like she was an actual doll.

PING!

The elevator opens. It takes all the restraint he has not to storm down the corridor and barge through the door. Best not to make a scene before he has to. He swipes his keycard, the door unlocks, but as Honeybear pushes it, the security chain snaps taut.

"Two seconds," Babydoll calls out, and her Honeybear doesn't like the tremor in her voice one bit. He can hear her play time playlist faintly through the door, Lil Mariko boasting about being a slut.

"Hon-um, Clint?" Babydoll checks.

"Yeah, Lulu, it's me..." the chain comes off, and the door opens. "Shit..." She's naked and trembling, with spats of blood across her face and chest. Staring as though she sees for miles, Babydoll doesn't seem aware she's still naked and stands exposed in the doorway, hands balled into fists.

"Je-," remembering where they are, he lowers his voice, "Jesus, what happened?"

Babydoll doesn't say anything and flinches as her Honeybear tries to take her in his arms.

"Shh, Babydoll, it's me," he reassures her, trying again, only slower, holding his arms open, inviting her to come in. Honeybear closes the door gently behind him as Babydoll steps into his embrace. Her breathing turns to scattered spurts as he wraps his arms around her, running his fingers through her hair, pressing her slight form tight.

"Shh, Babydoll, it's okay." She's his Babydoll, and no matter what, he's going to make sure she's ok. "It's gonna be okay." Whatever's happened, whatever this guy did to her, they'll deal with that in time. If he's wronged her, he'll pay, but right now, she needs to know her Honeybear's there, and so that's what he does – till she's ready to show him.

"Shit," Honeybear says when he sees the body.

He thought maybe this guy got too rough and his Babydoll hit back. That he ran off before help arrived. But there he is, facedown, unmoving, with what

Honeybear has to admit is a pretty impressively toned ass on full display. It's the wrong time for it, but all Honeybear can think is how unfair it is that his butt has fucking dimples. If his Babydoll wasn't a quivering bag of nerves, he'd be inclined to high-five her for nabbing such a choice catch. And if it weren't for the nail file jutting out of the guy's neck, Honeybear would have said his Babydoll fucked him into a coma. It wouldn't be the first time.

There's a dark, sticky wet patch up top, around the guy's neck, almost in line with a lighter one further down. Looks like things started well, at least.

Honeybear wraps his Babydoll in her robe and sits her on the room's single armchair.

"You need to tell me what happened, Babydoll," he says gently but firmly.

"W-we-we were fucking, and h-he saw my phone." She grabs her phone from the nightstand.

"Phone?"

Babydoll struggles to unlock it, can't keep her finger from twitching on the sensor. Eventually, she manages it, the screen lights up faintly. "You a-always wanna watch, so I thought I'd make a v-video." She holds the phone for her Honeybear to see. "For your birthday."

"Aw," he hugs her with one arm, "Babydoll, that's so sweet."

"Just watch," she hits play.

It starts with her carefully resting the phone against something; from the faint waves of white along the edge of the frame, Honeybear guesses she hid it with her shirt.

On-screen: Babydoll skips over to the bed and lies down, topless but still in her thong and heels. She props herself up on one elbow, crosses her legs, and blows a kiss at the camera to the sound of the bathroom door opening off-screen.

"Hi," on-screen Babydoll says over the top of the camera, looking at her playmate like she needs something to chew, and he's a big old pack of Juicy Fruit.

"Hey, Lil Lulu," Clint says as half of the frame fills with the guy's peach and Babydoll writhes on the bed. She sprawls and stretches like a kitten, giving him lots to look at.

Clint crawls on the bed, lean muscles flexing as he holds himself over Babydoll's waist and kisses her stomach. She giggles, bites her lip, and looks into the camera as Clint moves up her arched stomach.

Babydoll taps the screen and skips the video ahead.

"Hey, I wanted to see that," Honeybear complains.

"Sorry," Babydoll says and lets the video play.

On-screen: she's still on her back, though her knees are up, and she cranes her neck. The guy sits across her shoulders, straddling her, holding onto the headboard for balance as Babydoll's head rocks back and forth, working his cock like she's never heard of the term gag reflex.

Honeybear's throat goes dry at the sight of this guy's cock pushing against Babydoll's cheek from inside her mouth. Clint rolls his hips, swirling himself around Babydoll's mouth, and for every beat, Honeybear's heart skips; it beats for two on the next. "God bless 4k cameras," Honeybear moans.

On-screen, Clint's dick flops out of Babydoll's mouth with a pop, landing on her face with a wet slap. She giggles, stroking the thing with one backward curving hand.

"Fuck me, it's as big as your head," Honeybear whistles.

"Fuck me, it's as big as my head," on-screen Babydoll chuckles.

"Hah," Honeybear laughs, "jinx."

Though that makes a nervous smile flicker on Babydoll's face, she wants to get this over with, so she skips on again.

On-screen now, Babydoll's legs dangle in the air on either side of Clint's ass, her heels now gone and her pedicured toes curling in delight. Clint thrusts away, his balls clopping against Babydoll in rhythm with his grunts and her high-pitched squeals. She sounds so different, cumming from another man's dick. Not better, not worse; it just hits different. Honeybear's only heard it before when she "accidentally" called him while getting drilled one afternoon. "Accidentally," as she was pretty vocal about him for someone who didn't know her boyfriend was listening. That was both the quickest he's ever cum and taken someone off speakerphone. Neither are things you want to happen on a train ride.

Babydoll skips the video again, and now she's on her back, legs completely vertical. Her body, a reverse L shape with her legs crossed at the ankles. Clint holds her by said ankles, one hand big enough to wrap around both, and Honeybear watches the guy slide in and out of her at a steady pace.

"Woah," despite the situation, he's as hard as a rock.

Babydoll wipes a tear. "I thought you would like that."

"God damn, Babydoll, that's impressive," Honeybear clicks his tongue. Clint's packing some impressive inch-age, and Babydoll takes the whole thing. It's like a magic trick. She groans, and it's gone, sighs, and there it is again.

Babydoll skips again, and now she's looking right into the camera close-up. She moves back and forth, hair falling over her eyes as she bites her lip. Her eyes roll with each thrust and then find their way back to that defiant, dead-on stare.

Clint moans, loud, and he falls on top of her, pushing Babydoll forward till her head fills the shot. Her lips part with exaggerated surprise. "He just came in me," she mouths silently and blows another kiss.

Clint kisses her sweat-slick shoulder blades, and then, as he looks up, he too stares right into the camera. The idea of Clint looking in his eye, even by proxy, makes Honeybear throb, but the thrill only lasts for a second. Clint's face screws up in confusion that turns to anger.

"What the fuck?" Clint curses and clambers off Babydoll.

"Wait!" she protests as Clint grabs the phone.

"You're filming this!? Who do you work for, you fucking whore!?"

"It's not what you think –," everything swirls as the phone's tossed. There's a loud thud, and everything goes black as it lands face down on the floor, but it keeps recording.

"Please! No!" Babydoll's voice begs, and Honeybear tenses up. The thought that she went through this cuts him deep. He knows his love's alive and safe, next to him, but still. It makes him wish the guy was still alive so he could fuck him up himself.

She gargles. Motherfucker's choking her and not in the *do it daddy* way she sometimes likes. Things clatter, then there's an *oof* sound followed by gasps of shock.

"No…no – I didn't mean. I…no, oh god..." Babydoll's voice sobs and the real thing leans in closer, seeking shelter.

"Bitch," Clint says, only it comes out more like a spurt of sounds than a word. And then it's quiet.

"H-he thought I was making a sex tape to sell to the media," Babydoll explains, putting her phone to sleep.

"Why-oh shit!" Honeybear remembers where he saw Clint before. "That's that Olympic guy! The swimmer, right? Shit, that's where I got the name from now. How about that?"

"Yeah," Babydoll nods, "I was gonna ask you if you wanted to eat an Olympic swimmer's cum outta me?"

"Aw, Babydoll," Honeybear wraps both arms around her, pulling her to his chest. "I'd have said, well duh, wonder if his little swimmers will go for a podium finish too."

Babydoll snickers. "You always know what to say. I love you, Honeybear."

"God damn baby!" Honeybear kisses the top of her head, "I love you, too."

Babydoll looks at the body on the bed, "It was an accident. I didn't mean to, but he hit me and thought I grabbed the spray. You know, you always tell me to keep one by the bed just in case."

Honeybear looks at the nail file buried deep in Clint's neck.

"Easy mistake."

"I killed him!"

"And he deserved it!" Honeybear holds his Babydoll so he can look her in those near-black eyes he can just lose himself in. "I don't care if he gave you the ride of your life. Anybody lays hands on my Babydoll she doesn't ask for, and he gets what's coming."

Babydoll smiles and kisses her Honeybear. It's right there with that goofy smile and warm eyes framed by floppy hair as always. Just that is enough to let her know her world hasn't collapsed away beneath her feet.

"What are we gonna do, though? Should we call the police?"

The scandal, even if it is self-defense as the video would prove, they'd be outed. Babydoll's career would be over; there's no way it survives that kind of tabloid feeding frenzy and twitter outrage. No, they've got to play this like they always do. Down low.

"Don't worry, Babydoll; we'll take care of this ourselves."

"How?"

"Well, first, let's get him to the bathroom before he bleeds over everything."

"Olympic swimmer, dead in the shower, now that's a headline," Honeybear tries to lighten the mood as he lays Clint's body to rest inside the walk-in shower. He can see the faint outline of his Babydoll flitting around through the frosted glass.

"That's not funny!" she yells.

"I mean, kinda," Honeybear says to Clint's dead eyes, "am I right, buddy?" He holds out for a fist bump that Clint, understandably, doesn't return. "Dude, cold! Bone a guy's chick and not even a fist bump? Rude."

Honeybear's stripped down to his pineapple print

boxers, more to keep any blood off his clothes than because he's horny, though the bulge out front doesn't exactly discount that possibility.

Clint bled more as they moved him, but now only a few small red trickles seep out around the nail file; it pokes out like an antenna. Honeybear tenses a finger against his thumb, trying to resist the urge to ping it.

"What now?" Babydoll asks from the door, stripped down for the same reasons.

"I don't –,"

"Fuck bitch lie cunt!" Clint's body lashes, reaching out toward the couple with a swipe that's way off before he slumps back into a silent stupor.

"Fuck a duck; he's alive!" Honeybear gasps.

"What are we gonna do!?" Babydoll panics.

Clint's hand flops on the tiles like a fish stranded ashore.

"No, no, this is good," Honeybear nods. "Yeah."

"How!? He's gonna go to the police!"

"Is he?" Honeybear thinks it over. "For one, we have his sex tape slash evidence of him assaulting you, and he sure as shit didn't want anyone to see the first part of that. Gotta imagine he's not too chirpy about his fans and sponsors seeing the rest either."

"Yeah, but if it gets out, I'm –,"

"It's not gonna, though. He thinks you're Lulu?"

"Yeah?"

"And you never took your wig off?"

"Uh-huh."

"Cool! I booked this place using the playtime card, and neither of us brought our real phones?"

"Of course."

"So, there's nothing to trace this to us. Let's clean up and bolt."

A fresh gush of blood ebbs around the nail file like an oozing zit. It flows down Clint's neck, running to his lithe, muscular chest in starkly contrasting rivulets. His outburst must have disturbed the wound as more darkly red tendrils join it.

"Though we better get a move on." Honeybear eyes the wound. "He's not gonna last the night."

"They never do..."

Honeybear's eyes go wide at the joke. He slowly turns, one eyebrow arching as he locks stares with Babydoll. She leans against the doorframe; one arm crossed over her chest and the other up to her mouth as she bites on her thumb, suppressing a giggle. It takes a second for him to crack. He smirks, she loses control, and then they're both laughing while Clint's mouth bobs silently. Almost like he's in on it.

Funnies aside, there's still the matter of the dying guy. It was easier when they thought he was already dead; this makes things more complicated. They can't just leave him to die, can they?

"What do you need me to do?" Babydoll asks.

"Get our shit together, I'll figure this out."

Honeybear waves his hand dismissively at Clint. "Gimme your curlers, though."

"Ok?"

"And your phone, too."

"Why?"

"I wanna watch the video again."

"But... I nearly killed a guy in it..."

"Yeah," Honeybear takes Babydoll's hands, looks her in the eye, and says, "and you looked so fucking hot doing it, too." He kisses her, and then they get to work.

"Ok, here goes," Honeybear stands over the body with the smoking curling iron in one hand, the other hovering over the nail file. "Just pluck it and cauterize the wound; that'll stop the blood and keep the guy from bleeding out till help comes, right?"

Honeybear pumps himself up and then yanks the nail file – it breaks in two instead of coming out, leaving a small shard of metal sticking out of the guy's increasingly paler skin. "Dammit!"

"What!?"

"Nothing, Babydoll, I got this," Honeybear

answers sweetly and then turns back to the body. "You goddamn asshole!"

He thinks about what to do and then calls out to Babydoll, "Hey, snookums, you got tweezers in that mobile warehouse of yours?"

"Uh, sure, but I didn't say you could jack-off yet!" She titters, clearly thinking she's funny.

"Babydoll, you know that's not..." Honeybear can't deny, it's pretty funny, "good one. Ok, yeah."

She reappears in the doorway and holds out a tiny pair of tweezers. The robe's back on, but she's not bothered to fasten it. She holds the tweezers out with a wicked, lip-biting smile. Honeybear reaches for them, and Babydoll pulls back, teasing with another giggle.

"Babydoll, as cute as your evil little brat stuff is, and believe me, I'm saving all these spankings you're earning for later," Babydoll makes an O-face at that, "if I don't hurry your broken toy here's going in the trash."

It really should shock them more that they're thinking of this guy as a thing, but plenty of experience seeing random dudes as living sex toys coupled with the nervous bubbling energy brought on by shock has both Babydoll and Honeybear just on the functional side of hysteria.

"Fine," Babydoll hands them over with a pout.

"Ok," Honeybear tilts Clint's head to the side, exposing his neck and the half-inch of metal jutting out like sterling silver stubble. Honeybear squints and pokes his tongue out the corner of his mouth as he focuses. "This would be so much easier if it wasn't so small."

"Licking his balls earlier helped with that," Babydoll offers.

"You wanna get in here and give it a shot?" Honeybear teases, but the groan Babydoll makes and the way his cock throbs at the very mention of it doesn't feel like a joke. "Can you hold his head?"

"I don't think we should be playing right now, Honeybear."

"I mean his actual head. Honestly, girl, can you get your mind out of the gutter for five minutes?"

Babydoll steps over them and squats, holding Clint's head in place.

Honeybear checks the heated curling iron is within reach and then leans in again, this time trapping the tiny shred of metal between the sharp edges of the tweezer.

"Gotcha, fucker," he quietly smirks and slides the shard out. It comes with fresh bubbles of dark red blood pulsing around it, almost drowning the broken file, making the tweezers almost too slick to get the job done.

"Fuck yeah!" Honeybear cheers and tosses both tweezer and broken file down. He grabs the curling iron as Clint's neck and shoulder washes red, then brings the iron down fast.

Flesh sizzles and wafts of smoke nearly obscure Honeybear's vision as the scent of something like sweet barbecue marinade burning fills the shower room.

Clint's eyes rip open wide with raw fury.

"Shit!" Honeybear leans back as the guy takes a swipe at him, pulling the curling iron away with strings of seared flesh and a crumbling coating like it's been deep-fried red batter.

Clint lashes out with a desperate lack of focus. Hands swinging at where Honeybear used to be and then at nothing at all.

Babydoll shrieks and makes herself small in the corner.

The sound and sight of his girl so scared fires Honeybear up, and he reacts. He swings the curling iron, clunks Clint across the head, and it comes away with a hiss, and a patch of smoking skin stuck to it.

Clint flops back, head smacking off the frosted glass wall, a line of flesh ripped clean from his temple.

"Shit! Sorry dude, you startled me."

Clint jerks as though in mid-seizure, and Honeybear freaks out again. He wails the guy with a high-pitched shriek, bringing the curling iron down right in the middle of his head. The force rips it from the cord, caves in a dent that hisses like a smoking crater, and Clint stares up at it, crossed eyes, tongue out like an eGirl pulling an ahegao face.

"What the fuck!" Babydoll screams, backed as far away she can get from the scene. "Is he dead?"

Honeybear looks at the guy with the Remmington unicorn horn and watches for any sign of life. Just to be sure, Honeybear leans in and prods one of Clint's glazed-over eyeballs. Quickly, like poking a fresh wound, and when there's no response, he does it again.

"I would say so."

"What the fuck just happened?"

"He attacked," Honeybear states like it's just a thing that happens. "And I guess I killed him."

"You too, huh?" Babydoll can't help herself and, not for the first time this evening; her Honeybear remembers why he loves her so much. Her fucked up matches his crazy like two pieces from different jigsaws that somehow click. He can't help it, he laughs, and before she knows it, his Babydoll joins in.

"Is he dead-dead?" She asks, "cause we thought so already."

Honeybear checks for a pulse. "Yep."

"What are we gonna do?"

"The plan still works; we just don't have to hurry anymore..." Honeybear loses his train of thought as Babydoll rises to her feet. Since he's on the floor, she towers over him, and he admires the view. Her robe still hangs open, and his eyes follow her warm-toned legs up to her thigh gap, to her puffy and raw pussy lips still pouting from the hard fucking she took only a short while ago. He spots silvery splattering of dried cum on the inside of her thighs, and that sets his mind ablaze about where the rest of it will be. That what's inside her is more alive than the body it came from.

Honeybear's eyes continue up, across her toned stomach and small swollen and blood speckled nipples to those gorgeous black eyes that stare down at him. She's a goddamn goddess, and all he wants is her to fuck him up right now.

"What?" Babydoll asks and tucks a loose strand of her wig behind her ear.

"You're so fucking beautiful." He should feel guilty, right? He just killed a guy, but all he can think about is how perfect his girlfriend looks, standing there covered in some other guy's blood. His cum still swishing inside her sweet, freshly-fucked pussy.

"Stop simping, we gotta get this cleaned up."

"Yeah...," that's a good idea, Honeybear thinks. A hell of a good idea. "What if... I said I wanna eat you out right now."

Babydoll squints.

"How often am I gonna get the chance to clean a dead guy's cum out of you?"

Babydoll only stares in response. It's impossible to tell if she's into it or grossed out. There's a surprisingly fine line between both.

"Lemme clean it all up, Babydoll?" Honeybear stares up, pleading with those soft, kind eyes framed by half-moon whites.

Babydoll doesn't know what to say. She sees his sincerity – not to mention the bulge in his shorts.

"Really?" she asks, warming to the idea, getting a little excited by it.

"Absolutely," Honeybear says and shuffles towards her on his knees. He kisses her thigh while one hand caresses her backside and gently urges her to lift a leg.

"I, um," Babydoll bites down the twinge that it sends through her. "This is nasty," she protests, yet leans in with one knee. Honeybear takes her cue, lifts her leg, and rests it over his shoulder; her toes point daintily as her boyfriend kisses a line inside her thigh.

"Icky," Babydoll closes her eyes and grabs onto Honeybear's hair for balance. "Filthy," she gasps and pushes herself onto his face harder. Using her hooked leg, she forces him to kiss her pussy, and just as she's about to let go, her eyes land on the dead man, slumped in the corner, staring up with crossed eyes. "Wait!" Babydoll pushes back.

"Huh?" Honeybear looks at her, lips all sticky.

Babydoll looks from the dead guy to her boyfriend.

"Fuck it!" She grabs Honeybear again and shoves his head back into her crotch. "I love it!"

Babydoll grinds her hips to help, driving her pussy hard against Honeybear's face, her clit smashing against his smushed nose. One hand goes to her chest, slipping inside the robe, and she pulls on one of her piercings till it hurts. The whole time she doesn't break eye contact with Clint's glassy stare. She's never been reclaimed in front of the playmate before, and dead or not, she's into it.

Honeybear's tongue works at her, lapping with its full breadth, parting her lips. He tastes warm wetness, cold sweat, and as he curls inside her, the salty tang of a dead man's cum. He guzzles it like a thirsty man given a drop of water. His tongue can't possibly go as deep inside his Babydoll as Clint's cock, but that doesn't mean Honeybear's not gonna try. Babydoll's been a dirty girl and it's her Honeybear's job to clean her up, after all. So, he sucks, drawing out the sticky, stingy nectar of the dead man and his girlfriend's mixed fluids.

"I can taste him," Honeybear gasps in between breaths heavy with the scent of spit and cum.

"Oh-my-god," Babydoll pants, hearing that almost makes her lose balance. "Stop-stop-stop!"

Honeybear tears himself away from her clit and looks up. "You ok?"

"Yeah," Babydoll catches her breath. She flushed, coated in a sheen of fresh sweat, and all she did was stand there getting eaten out. "Oh, yeah."

Honeybear stands up and reaches to wipe his glistening chin.

"Don't," Babydoll grabs his hand. "It's disgusting." She steps to him, goes on her tiptoes, and licks from Honeybear's chin to his lips. "I love it!" And she kisses him, hungry for the tang of Clint's cum on her boyfriend's tongue.

"How's that taste?" Honeybear asks like he can read her mind. Or he just knows how fucking filthy his Babydoll truly is.

"Like I want more," Babydoll growls.

"More?"

"Yeah," she doesn't hesitate, "fuck me over him,"

Babydoll orders as she tears her robe off.

"You serious?" Honeybear smiles like it's Christmas morning.

"Oh, yeah," Babydoll paws at his shorts, finger pressing into a newly emerging sticky wet spot at the peak of Honeybear's tent. "Don't you wanna?" She gives him that bitey-lipped-black-eye smile he could never say no to, even if he wanted. "Fuck me over his corpse."

Seconds later, one of Babydoll's palms slams against the frosted glass wall, right across a streak of drying blood. The other grips Clint's shoulder, and she lifts her butt invitingly.

Honeybear pulls down his shorts and, if he's honest, he's a little jealous. He's always wanted Babydoll to fuck on top of him, bracing herself against his shoulders as some dude drills her. Seeing her eyes roll back, warm breath hitting his face as she cums. Even though he's dead, Clint's about to get one hell of a show.

Babydoll strokes Clint's cheek and turns his head, making his eyes roll and land in her direction like bingo balls falling into the slot. She stares into those vacant eyes as her Honeybear slides into her.

"Oh, hey there, Honeyboo," Babydoll almost goes cross-eyed as her Honeybear fills her up. He's usually rock hard for hours after she fucks another guy, but this is something else. Who knew manslaughter was such an aphrodisiac? Damn, she hopes there's still some left inside. She loves the idea of her Honeybear's dick pushing through another man's cum, of him shooting into her too, both loads mixing, dripping out of her like stirred honey for her hungry bear.

"Grab his junk," Honeybear orders as he picks up speed; one hand covers hers on the glass – fingers intertwined – as the other grips her bicep, holding her in place.

Babydoll obeys. She doesn't have to worry about being rough, not that she would anyway, but there's something to being able to squeeze as tight as she wants — watching the skin bulge between her fingers like a stress ball. She twists it, meshing both parts and digging her nails in.

Again, the pang of jealousy. She knows he wants her to kneel on his cock while she sucks some guy off. This feels like an attack, and Honeybear uses that to fuck her harder. She loses her grip as her body slams against Clint's. Honeybear's cock pops out of her as she goes, and she lands on Clint's cold, dead, limp dick.

"Wait," she says as Honeybear shuffles forward on his knees to pick back up. "I've got an idea." She climbs off the body and tries to drag it to lie flat. "Help me?"

"What you thinking?" Honeybear asks, casually stroking his dick as he watches his naked girlfriend struggle to move a dead body nearly twice her size.

"I want you to fuck me on top of him," Babydoll says, and her Honeybear doesn't need to hear anymore. They drag the body till it lies flat, and Honeybear watches with the biggest smile as his Babydoll steps over it, then lowers herself.

She takes Clint's soft yet still significant package –

guiding it up so that it rests against her clit – then sets down with enough pressure to hold it in place despite how wet she is.

Honeybear climbs behind her. He re-enters and begins to thrust, pushing her body up along the dead man's shaft.

She looks into his vacant eyes and licks the blood from his lips. The feeling of the dead guy's cock outside, her boyfriend's inside, both grating against her, makes her lose all sense of coordination. She grinds against both, like some awkward dance, never relenting for a second. The shower room fills with the echoes of breathy pleas for more and the slapping of balls on balls.

Babydoll cums, grabbing a fistful of Clint's hair to keep herself from collapsing, ripping a clump free.

Honeybear shoots into her, the sudden increase in pressure making it impossible to stop even if he wanted to, holding her flush to his body as his cock pumps over and over, filling her up till it seeps out around them.

Babydoll feels him slip free and dribbles escape her pulsating hole, spattering the corpse below before she can reach down and stop it.

"Shit," Honeybear says as he reclines, sweat glinting on his forehead.

"That was amazing," Babydoll adds as she fights quivering thigh muscles to stand, holding a hand across her pussy to stop anything else spilling out. It's a little too late for that. Clint's bruised groin is slick with her juices and a splattering of Honeybear's cum.

Babydoll rubs her sticky hand across Honeybear's face, smearing the mess across his cheeks and then finger-fucking his waiting mouth, and her Honeybear eats it all up.

"How's that taste?" she giggles.

"Disgusting," he says and grabs her by the wrist. He kisses her fingers, sneaking licks of what little dollops of milky white goo remain till she's all clean. "And I fucking love it."

The sink runs, and they clean up as much as they can with a dead body still in the middle of the shower room.

In the post-fuck glow, as the reality of their situation comes down sans the hormonal high, they're left with the realization they've just gotten some very incriminating DNA over this corpse.

"The fuck we gonna do about this body now, though?" Honeybear asks.

Babydoll looks to both men, the living and the dead one, and wonders out loud, "do you think a dead guy can get hard?"

Honeybear smirks. "Took the words right outta my mouth."

The Morning After...

———————|———————

Everything fucking hurts.

There's a single sliver of light coming through a crack in the blinds cutting through dank air, heavy with the stale stink of sex, sweat, and a rich metallic twang. The light falls on Honeybear's eyes, burning like a laser. He turns, grumbling incoherently, and clings desperately to the last threads of sleep. It's futile, though, and now that he's half-awake Honeybear's bladder is like, *move, bitch, I gotta go!*

"Ah, fuck it," Honeybear accepts defeat and finds the strength to pry his eyes open. Mistake. The tiny dose of morning wakes him up faster than a dry dildo up the ass.

Babydoll lies next to him, on her side, wigless with all those rainbow strands covering half her face like a clown's mop. She's done that thing she always does where she takes all the covers, then tucks most of them under her, meaning most of her body's exposed. There's a little pool of drool on her pillow, and her legs jerk every couple of seconds.

"Aw, are you humping in your sleep again?"

Babydoll's nose twitches, and Honeybear leans over, kissing her cheek. He throws in a gentle and loving pat on her exposed butt, too.

"We gotta get up soon though, you sleepy, slutty little kitten."

Babydoll snores. The timing is suspiciously perfect, making Honeybear narrow the one eye he can bear to open.

Getting up isn't going to be an easy or smooth operation. For one, Honeybear's ass feels like it's on fire. He has a vague recollection of his Babydoll reverse cowgirling Clint's body while she made him bend over, slapping him with - oh God, not again.

Gulping, which only makes his asshole hurt more, Honeybear reaches down, touches his butt cheek, and bites his lip as his fingers find something cold and metal parting them.

"No?" Honeybear winces as his hand wraps around the handle of Babydoll's curling iron, buried in his ass. His finger accidentally squeezes the lever, causing the metal grip inside to stretch his rectum.

"Oh, this is gonna suck." Honeybear bites down on his pillow and takes a firm grip. He shoots one bloodshot eye at his Babydoll and once again marvels at how convenient it is she could sleep through a car crash; he doesn't recall giving her permission to ram a bloody murder weapon up his butt.

"Three, two-motherfuck!" He yanks on two, trying

to surprise himself, and the iron comes out with two puffs of foul air. Well, that's one way to make a stuffy room stagnant with the unique bouquet of blood, cum, and death even more pungent.

Babydoll groans in her sleep, hand slapping at her nose.

"Oh, like you don't sleep toot," Honeybear growls and slides his way off the bed, not quite ready to place his butt down on anything yet. He holds the iron at arm's length and doesn't even want to look at it. Even if he hadn't used it to brain Clint, there's no way they're keeping this thing now and…

"Oh shit," it hits Honeybear; they just might have crossed a line last night.

With great debauchery, there must also come great regret. For if there's no shame, then where's the fun?

It's always the same combination of doubts, regret, and pride. Same as the very first time, when Babydoll sent a selfie of herself holding some stranger's cock with the caption saying she found Honeybear's porn bookmarks and wanted to double-check this was what turned him on. Same as when he came back to a hotel room to see Babydoll, all schoolgirl costume, and pigtails, on her back, arms hooked around her legs, keeping her pussy up in the air as the combined load of three men oozed out of her. No matter how tame the transgression, how extreme, things always feel different the morning after, and what they did last night, well, that's gonna be a conversation, to say the least.

For now, though, and till Babydoll decides to wake

up, Honeybear's got other things to deal with. Like the violent urge to pee, which he's gonna have to do sitting down. That whole region feels somewhat loose, like a luggage compartment after turbulence, and he doesn't quite trust himself.

Honeybear staggers towards the bathroom. He passes the mirror and does a double-take when he spots the curled wig on his head.

"Oh, shit —"

Honeybear flashes on being held by that wig, Babydoll pushing his head down to see a dead guy's shaft splitting her pussy lips, his rather impressive cock somehow swallowed to the balls by her narrow slit. He can't take his eyes off the wetness where his pale skin meets her olive, the way it wrinkles as she shifts from side to side, making the dead man's dick stir inside her.

"How's that look?" Babydoll teases. "You like seeing your girlfriend ride a big dick?"

"God Damn, I fuckin' love it, Babydoll," Honeybear moans, and she pulls him closer. All he can hear is the wet slurps of her pussy eating Clint's cock.

"How about when I do this?" Babydoll pushes up on her knees, sliding up Clint till just the head stays gripped between her shiny lips.

"Oh, fuck yeah," Honeybear bites his breath, on edge, hoping the dick stays in.

She slams back down, taking all of it again, making both Honeybear and herself grunt for entirely different reasons.

"Thank you," Honeybear smiles; there are almost tears in his eyes, "thank you for letting me watch."

Babydoll wiggles her hips. "Shouldn't you say thank you to Clint, too?"

"Dude, thank –"

"Ah-ah!" Babydoll interrupts, "say it to his dick."

"What?"

"Say thank you, Clint's dick, for filling up my girlfriend's tiny, wet pussy so well," she pushes down harder just for emphasis.

"Thank you, um, Clint's dick, for filling up my girl's sweet little pussy."

"You know what would be so hot?" Babydoll says as she slides up. "If you kiss my clit while he's in me!" She groans.

"Your wish," Honeybear cranes his neck, "my command." His lips graze her clit, and he feels her body twinge in response.

"That's good, Honeybear," she sighs, "kiss my fucking clit." She wiggles around, and his tongue slides across the line between pussy and cock. "Such a good boy, now-hey! What are you doing!"

Babydoll points between her Honeybear's legs as

he tugs away on his cock.

"Um, well, when a guy's horny, he sort of –"

"Did I say you could play with yourself?"

"Yes?" Honeybear raises an eyebrow in hope.

"Nu-uh, Honeyboo, I don't remember giving you permission."

"Aw, but Babydoll!"

She twirls her finger, telling her Honeybear to turn around.

"Baby –"

"Turn around! You've lost perving privileges!"

"Seriously?"

Babydoll stops riding the dead guy and gives her Honeybear full-on hands-on-hips stare. "I'm not gonna fuck him till you do what you're told." She pouts, hitting Honeybear with that little scrunch face that makes him weak.

"Fine," Honeybear tuts and shuffles around his butt like a petulant toddler. "'It's not fair."

"You know what's not fair?" Babydoll moans. "How good this dead guy's dick feels! Ohmygod!"

Honeybear rocks on the spot, whinge-moaning and grumbling incoherently.

"That's enough! You've been a naughty boy, and you need to be punished! Don't you?"

"Yes, Babydoll," Honeybear groans.

"Bend over and take it then."

Honeybear smirks and does as he's told – leaning over with his bare ass tipped within easy reach. Babydoll slaps once, hard, getting both cheeks, and Honeybear grunts.

"What was that?"

"Nothing," Honeybear insists.

"Thought so," she slaps again, then gets him with a follow-up backhand. Babydoll giggles at Honeybear's reddening cheeks and then her eyes drift to the floor. She spots something that makes her smile, something that gives her a wicked idea.

"Now, be a good boy, and I'll let you watch again," she says and picks the curling iron up.

Honeybear pulls the wig off and throws it toward the pile of clothes on the floor. He shakes his head and continues on to the bathroom.

Still half asleep, he pays no mind to the smears of blood across the dark hardwood floor, the scattering of red handprints leading up the wall by the door, or the conflation of them around the lock. Likewise, the fact that the door sits ajar is beyond his comprehension at the moment.

He lowers himself carefully, slowly, onto the toilet and hovers just an inch above. Even that hurts.

"Ah, fuck yeah," Honeybear sighs as he lets go and feels some of the tension escape. It provides him with a moment of clarity. One in which he makes two observations. The first is that his Babydoll is one sick, perverted little kitty, and he just wants to take her in his arms, kiss her and then hold her hair while she sucks some more dead guy's cock. The second hits as he looks around for something to wipe with. It's not just paper the bathroom is missing. There are splatters of blood on the frosted walls, sticky pools on the tiles, and a distinct lack of one dead Olympic swimmer. Did they move him at some point?

Some of the night is still fuzzy, but Honeybear's pretty sure they didn't take Clint out of the bathroom.

"Wait," he says as his eyes follow bloody footprints across the tiles, a handprint on the frosted glass wall. He follows the trail back out towards the front door, and it's a good thing he just went to the bathroom because as he realizes Clint's somehow got up and walked out of here, Honeybear just about shits himself.

"Where is ya," Clint stumbles down the hall, using the

wall for balance. "Where is the thing? What pancakes?" His hair pokes up like spiky little devil horns around a deep, weeping concave. He swings his arms, yelping, batting at nothing. Pee dribbles on the carpet, splashing his leg and trailing it as he staggers along.

"Baby… baby… baby!" Honeybear shakes Babydoll, trying to force her up.

"Stop-it-sleepy," she mumbles and slaps at him.

"Babydoll, you need to get up like right now!"

"No-sleepy-forever."

"Baby, I'm not kidding. We got a situation!"

She slaps at her naked little backside. "Do-what-you-gotta," she yawns, "just-don-wake-me-up."

"Babydoll I–" Honeybear's eyes land on round cheeks, all dimply and inviting in the morning light, like juicy olive tinted peaches just begging to be bitten. "Oh damn… no, shit, Baby, wake up! The dead guy's gone!"

Babydoll jerks awake, the back of her skull whams Honeybear's nose, launching him off the bed. She scrambles to her knees, and Honeybear's palm slaps on the bed, pulling the rest of him up with a trail of blood running from his nose.

"Did you say Clint's gone!?"

"Yeah!"

"Then what the hell you still doing here? Go find him!" Babydoll waves Honeybear on while her eyes dart around the room. "I gotta find something to wear."

Clint's hand squeaks along the color-changing glass, leaving behind rusty red smears.

"Cfunnnapop," Clint mumbles and pauses, looking at nothing. "Whassamayip?" He squints like he can't understand a response. "Yip?" He shakes his head and moves on, waving off whatever hallucination he was talking to.

Honeybear skids out of his room Risky Business style and catches sight of Clint's bloodied bare butt cheeks jiggling slightly as he stumbles through the hall. It's not the time, but the fact that even an Olympian like Clint has a little wiggle to his waddle makes Honeybear feel a little better about his burgeoning love handles.

He runs after him, only realizing he's not got any pants on as his dick flops around, slapping his thighs.

"Hey there, Clint," Honeybear tries to take Clint's

arm, and he pulls away, jibbering and blowing spit bubbles. "Come on, big guy, don't ya wanna spend more time with… shit what's the name again – Lulu?"

"Lu!" Clint goes rigid like a dog who just heard the word v-e-t. "No-no-no!" He panics and tries to run, moving like a drunken puppet.

"Hey-hey-hey," Honeybear gets in front of him. "It's cool, man, we're not gonna hurt you... well, you know, more than we already have."

Clint begins to cry.

"Oh, come on, there's barely a man alive that wouldn't take a blow to the head just to get a whiff of my Babydoll's panties!"

"Aw!" Babydoll coos from the door to their room, "really, Honeybear?"

"'Course Babydoll. I bet if you sold them, you'd make a killing."

Babydoll's got her robe back on, rainbow hair pulled into quick, messy bunches just to keep it out of her eyes.

Clint hobbles on, slapping his hand against a door for balance, as he makes his way to a cross-section with the elevator.

Babydoll hurries along the corridor, looking from Honeybear to Clint, urging him to do something.

"The hell's going on out there!" A rather angry voice from the room yells.

"Oh, shit," Babydoll and Honeybear say together as heavy footsteps stomp towards the door. They look at one another, and an unspoken thought passes between them.

Honeybear rushes to Clint. He wraps his arms around the guy and whirls him around the corner gracefully, bringing his other hand up to his mouth as they turn.

Babydoll slumps her whole body, lets her eyes droop, and starts dramatically yawning at the sound of a chain being torn free on the other side of the door.

"I said the hell-oh?" The door opens, and a big, balding man stands in an ill-fitting robe and tube socks. His fury level dips as his eyes do the same, looking down on Babydoll as she stretches like a kitten. "Can I help you?"

"Ohmygod!" Babydoll acts like she's just so embarrassed she can't even. "I'm so sorry; I thought this was my room. I got locked out, and my boyfriend could sleep through an earthquake."

"Lies," Honeybear mutters in Clint's ear as he holds the struggling man back, inches from the others.

"It's-" the guy in the room says, and a nasal screech cuts him off.

"Hermy! Who is it!?"

"It's, um, just a wrong door, Light of my Life," the guy, Hermy, says and smiles at Babydoll. She flashes one back.

"I'm so sorry! I didn't mean to wake you!" Babydoll calls around him.

A half-second later, a woman barges past the man.

"Really! Honestly! What kind of – oh my gosh, it's you!"

Shit, Babydoll screams inside her head. She's not wearing her wig.

"Herm! Herm!" The woman paws at her partner, "that's-that's-that's-"

It's too late now. She's been made and there's nothing left to do but go with it. Babydoll waves, "Hiya, again so sorry…"

"Oh my gosh, don't be silly! Herm! Go get my phone!"

Shit! Babydoll dies internally.

"Can I just say our daughter loves you? She called her hamsters Himiko and Ren. Just adores everything you do. Even the, you know, the one with…"

"Yeah? Really!? Aw, thank you! Tell her that's so sweet, and she's awesome."

"You gotta be fuckin' with me," Honeybear groans and struggles to keep Clint still. He's a lithe, wiggly thing and his bare ass keeps rubbing against Honeybear's crotch. "Shuddup, it's just friction!"

"Can I get a selfie with you?" The woman asks, snatching her phone from her partner without a word.

"Um," Babydoll gestures to her robe.

"Just our faces? Please!? Our daughter will just die!"

It's such a bad idea but saying no will definitely signal something's up. "Sure," Babydoll shrugs.

"Oh my gosh! Thank you! Herm! Take our picture!" She slaps the phone back into Herm's hand. He takes it with the unquestioning obedience of a married man with a daughter.

The woman sidles up next to Babydoll, squats down so she can smush her cheek against hers and puts her arm around her shoulder. Babydoll throws up a peace sign and does the same.

"Say, Princess Bubblegum!" The woman says, and her partner takes the shot.

"You two comin' back to bed or what," a deep, male voice calls from the darkness of the room.

The woman laughs nervously, turning red, while the man rubs his bald spot.

"Sometimes you just need to cut loose, you know?" The woman smiles awkwardly.

"Hey, don't we all," Babydoll gives them two thumbs up and then finger waves as the couple closes their door. The second the lock bolts, she dashes around the corner and comes to a sudden halt at the sight of Clint bent over, with Honeybear on his ass.

"Hey! Don't start without me," she jokes.

"Very funny. Now if you're done schmoozing with your fans, little help?"

"You ever think it's weird there's only ever one chair in hotel rooms?" Honeybear asks as he ties Clint's ankles to said solo armchair. Babydoll works at his wrists, though Clint's not putting up much of a fight anymore, his ramblings replaced by random twitches, and he keeps staring up and then right.

"Kinda?" she says, doing that little face scrunch and realizes her Honeybear's got a point.

"Like, that bed easily fits four people."

"I'd say six at least," Babydoll says with a smirk.

"Damn, that's hot Baby," Honeybear holds out for a high-five, and Babydoll hits it. "I'm thinking it's the husband's chair."

"Huh?"

"Yeah, like whoever started this whole watching your partner bang thing was sick of peeking through a hole in the wall or whatever. Like, that can't be good for your back? So, he was like, fuck it, I want a comfy chair to beat off in while my woman's taking it face down, ass up."

Babydoll thinks about it for a second.

"It's the only thing that makes sense," Honeybear pulls the makeshift restraints tight. It's a good thing Babydoll brought her fluffy pink handcuffs; they didn't have enough robe belts to do all four limbs.

"You know, I'm not really seeing a fault in your logic, but that can't be it?" Babydoll puts a hand on one hip and tilts her head the other way. "Can it?"

"World's full of perverts just like us," Honeybear says with a knowing wave.

"Yeah! Oh! Guess what! That couple back there? Threesome, they had another dude back in the room."

"Shut! Up!"

"Yeah-huh!" Babydoll nods excitedly.

"Good for them," Honeybear feels validated and a little jealous. "I want a threesome."

"Aww, Honeybear," she goes to him, up on her tiptoes, and throws her arms around his neck. "How about next weekend?"

"Wait!? You mean it!? I can join in and…"

Babydoll laughs and playfully slaps her Honeybear's cheek. "I'm just fucking with you. No, you can stay home like a good boy, but I'll send you a selfie from the bathroom after." She kisses his cheek. "Now," she turns to their bound captive, "what are we gonna do about him?"

Clint mumbles and nods, like he's talking to someone. When he moves his head more vigorously, yellowish ooze seeps through his head wound, trickling down the caved-in hollow.

"I mean, I don't think he's gonna be able to identify us," Babydoll bites her lip. Something is stirring in her head that's definitely NSFW. She taps Clint's knee, and he swats in the opposite direction, backhanding Honeybear's dick.

"Ow!" He grabs his crotch, turning on the spot, dancing away the pain. "Why!?"

Babydoll giggles. "How could I know he'd do that?" She taps Clint's knee again, and his opposite hand flies off on its own, just like before. Honeybear dodges it this time.

"Quit it!"

Honeybear hits the knee closest to him, and Clint's other arm flies up, slapping Babydoll on the tit.

"Hey!" She rubs her boob. "That's not fun unless I'm horny!"

The implication of that makes Honeybear's brain slam on the break and rubberneck.

"You got your titties spanked?"

"Look, he spanked a lot of things before this," Babydoll holds her hands on either side of Clint's caved-in head. "Can we just focus on what we're gonna do with him?"

"Sorry," Honeybear scratches his head, the wig's itching him real bad. "Kinda hard to think when I'm turned on, you know?"

"Oh, sorry," Babydoll sighs sweetly, taps Clint on the knee, and shrugs as his opposite arm nails her Honeybear right in the junk again.

"Son-of-a-god-damn-bitch," he says through one prolonged, sharp intake.

"Might help if you put some pants on, you know? Instead of just shirt-cocking it like that."

"Fine," Honeybear moans and searches the pile of clothes on the floor for his boxers. Under the other man's shirt, he finds a phone he doesn't recognize. "Oh, shit, I think this is his phone." Honeybear picks it up. The screen is locked, but there are notifications. Multiple missed calls and unread messages. "Looks like people are trying to get a hold of your boy."

Babydoll crawls onto the bed, going on her knees so she can be the right height to look at the phone with Honeybear. He's sadly too preoccupied with the phone to enjoy the sight of her exposed butt cheeks, the robe doing nothing to cover them as she crawls.

"We should check it."

"I dunno, feels kinda wrong," Honeybear hesitates. "Going through another man's phone."

Babydoll hits him with a "seriously" look. Like that's the line they're not gonna cross.

"What?"

"Gimme that," Babydoll snatches the phone and tries to unlock it. No luck till she pops over, lifts Clint's limp hand, and puts his index finger against the sensor. The phone lights up.

"Why'd I never think to do that with your play phone?"

"I dunno," Babydoll stretches her foot while flicking through the phone, "I always kinda figured you did. You missed some spicy pics if you didn't."

"Aw, shit, really?"

"Yeah-huh," Babydoll bites her lip as she concentrates.

"Meh, I don't think I would have anyway. That's your space," Honeybear takes a seat on the bed.

"Aw, Honeyboo, you're too cute."

"Like, if you wanted me to see a photo of you with a mouthful of cum, you'd snap it to me."

"Ohmygod, I should do that!"

"Um, you did?"

"Did I?" Babydoll's face scrunches as she tries to remember.

"Oh, wait, it was the guy you were with. 'Cause he wrote something like, 'your girl swallowed it all after we took this.'"

"Oh yeah! Raoul," Babydoll bites her lip and looks up through the corner of her eye as the memory slaps her like the guy's cock did. She grunts, moaning as she recalls the taste of something tasty. "That was good. Cum doesn't always taste nice, but his was yummy."

Honeybear leans back on his elbows, looking his Babydoll up and down as light flickers across her face. She feels his eyes on her and looks up.

"What?"

"Just admiring what a gorgeous, greedy little sex kitten you are," he smiles. "And wondering what I did to get so lucky."

"Shut up," Babydoll sticks her tongue out. "Just 'cause I said some guy had tasty cum?"

"Among other things, yeah."

"Aww," Babydoll thinks for a second, "you tasted it too, though, so you know what I'm talking about?"

Honeybear squints. "No, you..." he corrects

himself. "Raoul sent that snap when I was away for that thing down south. Remember?"

"Oh, no, Honeybear, I fucked him at Mandy's baby shower. You were there, remember?"

"No?" Honeybear doesn't sound too sure.

"Check the Facebook photos," Babydoll smirks at something she sees on Clint's phone. "Awful lot of dick pics on here." Her own phone buzzes a second later.

"Did you just?"

"Nope." Babydoll feigns innocence. "Noooope," her phone buzzes again.

Honeybear's eyes narrow as he opens his phone and checks their old Facebook albums. "Son of a…" he says as he finds a group photo from that party. Babydoll's on her tiptoes, planting a kiss on him, and off to the side, a good-looking dark-skinned man is stroking his chin and trying not to laugh as he looks at them. "You even tagged him!"

Babydoll snort laughs, "Honestly, sometimes you make it too easy, Honeybear." She looks up, "Doesn't it make you wonder what other photos I'm sitting on?" Her eyebrows dance, "or what I'm sitting on in them?"

"God damn, I love you," Honeybear reaches for his crotch but stops as Babydoll tuts.

"Ok, so, I think we're good. He didn't send or share any photos of us together. I've deleted them from his phone, but we'll destroy it just to be safe."

"He had photos of you?"

"Yeah, I sucked him off in the bathroom." She

looks up at Honeybear's aroused silence. "What, you think I was gonna let that slut Ally upstage me? Bitch, please. Anyway, his coach and team's been looking for him. He told some of them he and I quote 'pulled this banging tight little Asian chick.'"

"Aw, that's not cool."

"Meh, lots of guys have a fetish. Works for me. Some of his buddies said some racist shit, but he verbally bitch slapped them."

"Aw, that's cool," he gives the tied-up, stupefied naked man a thumbs up. "Cheers, Clint."

"So, I think we're good. He's not gonna say anything about us, not after what we did to him, and there's no photos of us together anymore. I think we can just leave him, like you said, and things'll take care of themselves, right?"

"Except..."

"Except? Oh, shit!"

"Yup, you took a selfie with your fan next door; plus, there's bound to be security cameras in the halls. Right now, if anyone saw, they probably think it's just a drunken threesome. Bet they see all sorts of stuff like that all the time."

"Yeah, I met a guy in a hotel once and there was another hot wife in the lobby meeting before her gangbang at the same time."

"Really? That's hot," Honeybear laughs, "should have asked her if you both could join in."

"Who says I didn't? Anyway, we got another

problem then."

"What?"

"Look at the time, Honeybear," he checks his phone as Babydoll says it.

"Shit."

"Yeah, it's just under two hours till we gotta check out." Babydoll screws up her lip, "and I haven't even done my makeup yet."

Everything fucking hurts. Especially her pride.

Alana rubs her temples as the garish neon-pink lights of the lobby and deeply inconsiderate sunlight streams in through the window, both twisting into a migraine conspiracy currently assaulting her forehead.

Stupid, stupid Alana, drinking when you've got an early shift. Just a few drinks with the others. Oh, look who's sitting there at a table all alone, they say. Isn't that the cute guy you were crushing on, Alana? Maybe you should... yeah, that was a mistake. Besides, was he even that cute?

The elevator door opens, and there he is. Floppy hair falling over his soft brown eyes, smiling like a total doofus.

"Oh, fuck me," Alana groans. The guy looks like he's been up all night fucking, probably with his girlfriend. The slut. She bites back the bile and throws on a somewhat professional smile. "Ohayo! Good morning!

"Hey! Yeah, 'morning." Honeybear smiles and does that thing where he rubs the back of his neck again.

Stop that, Alana growls inside her head. It's too hard to hate you when you're so fucking cute.

"So, we were wondering if we could extend our stay?"

"Crazy night?"

"Like you would not believe! So, any chance?"

"I'll check." Alana looks through the incoming bookings on her tablet. There are enough open rooms to book him back in, but... why should she? So he can keep partying with his slutty girlfriend, who doesn't even seem to care she's got a hottie like him doting on her. *No, Alana, be professional.*

"We'd appreciate it. Seriously."

Fuck that.

"I'm sorry, sir, we're booked up," Alana says without looking up. "We're going to need the room back by eleven-thirty."

"Shit," Honeybear's heart drops. Alana takes a glance at him and then a double-take. He looks like she just told him his cat died or something. "There's nothing."

Do not feel sorry for him, Alana tells herself. Remember last night. Being nice isn't gonna get you anything. "Sorry, sir. We hope you enjoyed your stay at XOX. Arigato gozaimasu!"

"Fuck," Honeybear turns and heads back to the elevator. "Fuck, fuck, fuck."

Alana watches him make adorable little fists and slink away like a kid being told he can't have a new toy. That makes her feel a little better, restoring a shred of her dignity.

"Oh my god, Alana!" Another person, dressed in black, throws themselves on Alana's back. He squeezes her shoulders. Alana winces from both the volume of his voice and the enthusiasm of his grip.

"Ow, Bret, ow!" Alana complains and extricates herself. "Have you been drinking coffee with Red Bull again?"

"No, I mean, yeah, but that's not it. Come on, girl, there's something you gotta see!"

A couple of minutes later, Bret's dragging Alana into the dark, metallic security office where a bunch of black shirts stand around a monitor giggling, hands over mouths and eyes.

"Okay, she's here," one of them says, and another black shirt at the desk keys up a video on the monitor.

"What am I looking at?" Alana wonders aloud.

"Just watch." Bret can barely contain himself. He walks Alana through the crowd, pushing her till she has a good view of the screen.

"Oh, oh no," Alana starts to giggle as the black and white video shows two men, one fully naked and the other in just a t-shirt in one of the corridors. The one with the shirt's behind the naked one, arms around his waist, and it looks very much like he's taking the naked guy from behind. "Oh, no way."

"Isn't that your cutie-pie boy-crush?" Bret teases.

"Oh my god... it is."

"No wonder he turned you down then." Bret thinks for a second, then adds, "maybe I should have taken a shot?"

"It gets better," the black shirt at the desk says, hits a key, and the angle changes. Alana can see a tiny Asian woman in a way-too-short robe standing at the door around the corner from the two guys. She's chatting friendly and then goes into the room for a second. When she comes out, the girl darts around the corner, seemingly amused by the sight of the two men. She takes the naked guy's hand, and along with the shirt guy, they lead him back to their room.

"Oh. My. God." Alana's body rocks with laughter. No wonder he didn't mind his girlfriend being out partying; she was fishing for a guy for them both to fuck. It's so wrong and kinda hot, so it takes a moment before something else clicks. There's something not quite right with the naked guy.

"He's so drunk he doesn't even know where he is," Bret says, but Alana doesn't think that's it. They see all sorts of wild shit at XOX, the place sells itself as an upscale Japanese Love Hotel, after all, and there are all kinds of kinky shit going on all the time.

No, something about this doesn't feel right.

"I don't feel right," Babydoll rubs her arm, standing in the middle of the room like she's lost as Honeybear comes back in.

"What's the matter, Babydoll?"

She seems even smaller than usual, like she's shrinking in on herself under the weight of something horrible and oppressive.

"Did we rape him?"

"Oh," that hits Honeybear hard.

"We thought he was dead, but he wasn't, and I–" she falls into her hands, sobbing.

Clint's head darts around the room like a dog chasing a fly.

Honeybear goes to her, takes his Babydoll in his arms and strokes her hair. "I mean, first off, I didn't do anything to him, so—"

"Not the time! Jerk!" She slaps his chest.

"Okay, look, he was into it before, so maybe it's cool?"

"It doesn't feel right," Babydoll sobs. "I'm a

monster."

"No, snookums, no," Honeybear takes her at arm's length and looks into her watery eyes. "He put his hands on you! Tried to choke you, would have killed you. Far as I'm concerned, he got off light."

"Dry bees go vroom," Clint says, nodding like he agrees with Honeybear.

"See, he's cool with it?"

"I dunno," Babydoll scrunches half her face, looking at the naked, bloody man tied and handcuffed to the chair. "Why aren't we more freaked out?"

Honeybear shrugs. "You'd think we'd be more, but yeah… maybe, considering what we do for fun, we're just built different?"

"Built wrong."

"We can't have a pity orgy right now. We've got more immediate problems to deal with," Honeybear rubs his neck and breaks the bad news. "Can't extend our stay. So," he checks his phone, "We got an hour and change to deal with him.

"What are we gonna do?" Babydoll asks, though she knows the answer.

"I think we gotta kill him." It's not like he meant it when he brained Clint with the curling iron. "Like, properly this time," Honeybear gulps.

"I know." It's not like she meant it when she stabbed him with the nail file; he was choking the life out of her after all. "How are we gonna do it, though?"

"Maybe just a pillow over his head?" Honeybear

grabs one from the bed. It's stained with makeup and crusty spots. "I mean, it feels kinda boring, but it's gotta be the easiest way for us all, right?"

"Should we really be talking about killing someone as boring?" Babydoll points out. "Or easy?"

"How often are we gonna murder someone? Isn't our whole thing we're going to hell anyway –"

"So we might as well enjoy ourselves, yeah."

"Honeyboo, but I was talking about group sex and gloryhole stuff! Not killing someone!"

"I feel like it still applies." Honeybear catches what she said, "gloryhole?"

"Shit, I shouldn't have said that." Babydoll slaps her thigh in frustration as dots begin to connect in Honeybear's head.

"No, you didn't..." He says with hopeful exuberance, like he's looking at a wrapped gift that's very much in the shape of exactly what he wants.

"We don't have time," Babydoll complains, but Honeybear's already on his phone, opening a tab for PornHub. He opens his favorites, clicks on Glory Gang, and right there, the second most recent video: *Tiny Titty Asian Kitty Visits Glory Gang For Anonymous Orgy*.

"No, freakin' way," Honeybear's hand trembles with nervous excitement so badly he can barely hit play. It's only a teaser, with a banner directing to their website for the full three-hour-long video. "Three hours," just saying that makes him hard.

The clips plays and you wouldn't know it's Babydoll at a glance. The girl in the video has blonde pigtails; she half-turns to the camera, flashing a cheeky smile under a pink kitty masquerade-style mask.

"I'm so excited!" Masked-Babydoll giggles. "My boyfriend's a huge fan!" She skips ahead, letting the camera see she's only wearing wide pattern fishnets with no panties – the material cutting diamonds into her pert, olive cheeks – chunky white sneakers and a black crop top.

She prances through a room filled with naked guys, most of them up against walls where women's legs stick out through holes in all sorts of positions. Some stand with their legs apart, feet on the floor, others with them hooked into fabric stirrups up high. Music can barely be heard over the sounds of countless men and women moaning and enthusiastic, wet smacking.

Some guys stand around watching, waiting, and more than a few heads turn to watch Babydoll come in. She squeals with excitement, like a naughty kitty at Fuckland.

"Where can I go?" Babydoll asks, almost exploding with excitement, and the camera cuts away to an overhead shot. She's on her back inside a small, wooden room, lying on a black leather mattress. There are rope hoops for her to hold onto, and the bedazzled slogan on her crop-top, meow, catches the light. She reaches for the ropes and bites half her lip as her eyes pop.

The shot cuts outside, her legs are held up and

apart by black straps, showing that her fishnets are crotchless. One guy kneels before her, licking away at her pussy while another strokes her leg, kissing up and down it. The shot cuts back to Babydoll as she gasps, her body moving up along the mattress as she uses the hoops to pull herself back down. She lets go of one, lifting her crop top with it and playing with her pierced nipple.

Back outside, one of the guys has his pants around his ankles, one hand on a hip as he slides his cock in and out of Babydoll's wet pussy. He licks his other fingers, then reaches down and starts fingering her asshole. The second guy stands watching, waiting for his turn, jerking off.

The video jumps ahead. Babydoll is topless now and can barely hold on. It cuts back outside as the first guy moans loudly, saying something in Czech, and then pulls out. A clump of white goo seeps out of her shiny pussy and gets shoved back in as the second guy thrusts his cock into her. The camera cuts back inside as Babydoll cups both her breasts, stares right into the camera through her mask, and it fades to the company's logo.

"God. Damn." Honeybear stands erect in awe. "When did you–"

"When I did the European signing tour, but that's not important right now!"

"Just how much dick did you get on that tour?"

"I dunno, I lost count. Look, we can watch the full thing later and count them up, ok? We don't have time, and we really need to figure out how we're gonna... you know?" Babydoll tilts her head towards Clint as he stares like a butterfly just landed on his nose. "It's gotta be painless, clean. We don't want a mess."

"Yeah, like how messy your pussy was in that clip–"

"Can you not!" Babydoll slaps Honeybear's chest. "Think!"

"Ok," Honeybear takes a deep breath. "Ok-ok-ok... Baby, I got nothin'; I'm far too horny."

"Honeybear! Look, he's bleeding on the floor again!" Babydoll points to the wound on Clint's neck, it's been agitated with all the moving around, and dark blood seeps out through the yellow crusted pus.

"I gotta take care of this, Otherwise, I'm not gonna be able to think straight," Honeybear motions to his crotch.

"Urgh! Fine," Babydoll throws her arms in the air. "But make it quick."

"Would be quicker if you helped?" He floats the idea while wriggling out of his pants.

"What do you want?"

Honeybear thinks for a second. He likes the way she's just standing there in her robe, next to another man who's sitting there, staring, and the soft purple mood light coming off the frosted glass. It gives him an idea.

"Ok, you're a stripper whose boyfriend doesn't know and just caught you."

"You came up with that way too fast."

"I might have already had that one loaded."

"We'll come back to this one later, 'cause I think I know a place."

"Oh, shit!? Really!? Awesome!"

"You want me naked for this?" Babydoll starts untying her robe.

"Yeah, oh, and can you put your heels back on? 'Cause, you know, strippers and heels?"

"Fine. Do you want cute, slutty, or bitchy girlfriend?"

"Oh," Honeybear's spoilt for choice. "Bitchy. Go hard; that'll get me off quicker."

"No problem, Honeyboo," She ties her hair up. "Will you get the music? There's a playlist on my phone."

"Awesome!" Honeybear grabs her phone and opens Spotify. Her most recent playlist must be the one: *Songs to Cheat on My Boyfriend With*. "Cute," that makes him smile as he hits shuffle. It must have already been connected to the Bluetooth speakers as the whole room fills with a pulsing beat and Kesha's rawring.

Heels clack across the hardwood behind him, each step quick and proud. Honeybear turns around just in time as Babydoll slaps him hard across the face. He stumbles back into the wall as she grabs a fistful of his shirt.

"Are you stalking me!?" Babydoll demands.

"N-no," Honeybear protests, "I swear!"

"Don't lie! You think you can just follow me to work!?"

"I'm sorry–"

"You don't own me, you know? I can do whatever the hell I want with my body."

"Y-yeah, Baby…"

She slaps him again.

"I'm not your Baby while I'm working. I'm whoever's paying Baby. Is that clear?"

"Yes, perfectly clear. I'm so sorry."

"See that guy over there? He spends more money on my dances in a weekend than you make in a whole month. I mean, who do you think paid for that new Xbox?" She leans in and whispers in his ear. "Just remember when you're playing with yourself," she giggles, "that it was my tight little body that bought you the privilege. Loser."

"I'm so sorry Ba-I'm sorry!"

"You know you're lucky. He's turned on by the idea of you watching us. So, you're going to sit down," Babydoll pushes Honeybear till he's sitting on the floor, back to the wall. She puts one foot on his chest, digging the tip of the stiletto in. "And you're gonna watch how I earn the big bucks."

Babydoll kicks herself free from Honeybear, spinning on her heels. Her hands slide across her body as she crosses the room, moving along with the beat. She shoots Honeybear a smirk and flips him off in time, with Ashnikko singing how being a bitch is her kink.

Honeybear grabs his dick and starts working it, wet slapping noises and pre-cum splattering on his fingers as Babydoll parts her legs, keeping them straight and works her way down Clint's body. She keeps going till her ass is high, cheeks parting from the stretch. Honeybear can see her pussy and her upside-down head as she looks at him from between her legs, tongue out.

"Oh, fuck me," Honeybear cries out as Babydoll throws herself back, ponytail whipping, and then grinds down till she's kneeling in front of Clint. She climbs up his legs till it looks from Honeybear's perspective that she's giving Clint head.

"Sometimes they tip for extras," Babydoll teases as she turns around, leaning over till her ass is right in Clint's face. He seems to be paying attention to that, alright. "You know what the extras are? Right?" Babydoll asks as she slides her hands down her legs till she's touching her ankles.

Honeybear can't help but think about how many guys she's fucked in these ridiculously sexy shoes. He distinctly remembers her buying them and saying that it would be a crime not to be a slut with them right there in the middle of the store.

Babydoll climbs onto the chair with Clint. Honeybear can see his cock getting hard under her, and she glances over her shoulder. "And I get so many tips," Babydoll licks her lips as she pushes her pussy down closer to Clint's lap.

"Fuck!" That does it, Honeybear explodes,

shooting a load halfway across the room. He slumps deeper against the wall, catching his breath.

"Was that good, Honeybear?" Babydoll asks sweetly as she climbs off Clint.

"Fucking amazing, we gotta do this for real," he says, looking for something to clean up with.

"After we take care of this," Babydoll places one heel down, unknowingly, in the pool of fresh blood. "Now let's – Woah, Shit!" She slips, her ankle almost twisting as she loses her balance.

"Babydoll!"

She loses her balance, one of her heels breaks off, and she falls onto Clint. The momentum pushes the chair back, carrying them both with it.

THUD-CLUNK-CRACK!

"Babydoll!" Honeybear scrambles across the floor, his hand slips on his cum, and he plants his chin against the hardwood. "Fuck," he curses through a bitten lip, blood welling and running down his chin. "You ok, Babydoll!?"

"I'm ok," she crawls away to the side. "But, shit, look," she points towards the tipped chair.

Honeybear comes around the side and sees what she means. There's a bloody smear on the mounted half-table, but even without that, the fact that Clint's head sits at an impossible angle, neck all twisted and broken, would confirm that he's well and truly dead this time.

"It was an accident," Babydoll insists.

"Yeah," Honeybear agrees, "I guess that's that then." He holds his Babydoll close.

"Oh, you're hurt," she touches his bleeding lip, and Honeybear winces.

"It's fine; we've got less than an hour to figure out what we're gonna do with this body now."

"Yeah," Babydoll's at a loss.

"We got another problem too," Honeybear gulps.

"What is it?"

Holding Babydoll's naked body against his own, Honeybear answers. "I'm horny again."

C l e a n - U p   D u t y

———————|———————

"Enjoy your stay at XOX! Arigato gozaimasu!" Bret smiles through his teeth to a middle-aged, smartly dressed woman checking in on her own. She takes her keycard with a silent smile, and Bret holds his till she turns her back. The second the woman's out of earshot, he turns to Alana and mutters, "What do you think, married woman, having an affair?"

"You're obsessed," Alana says like she's not interested. "She's probably just in town for work or something."

"Uh-huh, yeah nobody's staying here for business unless it's business," Bret clicks and winks, "you feel me?"

"Not particularly."

"She had a tan line where a ring used to be, that's all I'm saying." Bret pretends to be suddenly interested in his tablet.

"You think maybe she's just gotten divorced? Or,

like, her partner died?" Alana says and then bites, "or maybe she's meeting a whole bunch of guys later on for a good old-fashioned afternoon deep-dicking gangbang?"

"Wouldn't be the first time," Bret smirks, "though nothing's beating two guys fucking in the hall while one's girlfriend covers with the neighbors."

"Don't, just don't," Alana groans. "I made a fool of myself with him."

"I wonder." Bret smiles as he imagines something. "They still checked in?"

Alana taps a few screens, "yep."

"They're cutting it close. Bet they're still fucking."

"Bret! Jesus Christ!" Alana smirks to herself, but Bret catches it.

"What you smiling about?"

"He may have tried to extend their stay, and I may have told him we're fully booked."

"Alana!" Bret gasps, "no, you didn't!"

She doesn't answer but can't hide the smirk.

"You're so wrong! I love it."

Alana shrugs playfully.

"I wonder what they're doing right now." Bret bites his finger as he pictures it. "Do you think she just watches the boys fuck, or is it like a threesome kind of deal?"

"I don't think I wanna know," Alana rolls her eyes.

"You sure?" Bret holds up his keycard. "I mean, wouldn't be the first time hospitality walked in on something... remember that time with the guy tied down, coke bottle stuck in his ass?"

"I don't want to! Believe me. Anyway, we can't," Alana tries to talk herself out of it, "we're on check-in till this afternoon."

"Easy," Bret whistles to another black shirt walking through the lobby. "Sammie, mind covering for us for a," he motions like he's smoking.

"No worries," the other black shirt comes over and takes Bret's tablet from him.

"Okay, girlie," he grabs Alana's hand and drags her to the elevator. As the door opens and he pushes her in, Bret adds, "let's go gate crash some freaky perverts."

"Ugh, the things I let you talk me into," Alana moans.

"Quit lying; you wanna see some kinky shit just as much as me. We're all sick fucks."

"I guess," Alana laughs. "I feel sorry for who actually has to clean up that room, though."

"Come on, we gotta clean this up like yesterday!" Babydoll scurries around the room, shoving clothes and makeup palettes into her case. She's got her underwear on now, the normal kind, not the too-sexy-not-to-be-seen-in-kind. "Wait, why are you taking your pants off?"

Honeybear pauses with his jeans by his knees. "So I don't get his blood on my clothes, duh."

"Yeah, that's smart," Babydoll goes back to stuffing her bag and, seconds later, her slutty senses go off. She raises her head, detects horniness in the air, and without looking back she snaps, "quit playing with yourself!"

"I can't help it!" Honeybear's got his hand on his dick, once again shirt-cocking it. "You're just so hot!"

"You just came."

"Yeah, but you know I always got some baby batter ready for you, snookums."

"Keep calling it that, and it's never coming on, or in me, again."

Honeybear grunts, "That's hot."

"Seriously!" Babydoll throws her arms in the air. "How about figuring out what we're gonna do with him!" She points to the body on the floor, tied to the chair with a broken neck. "How are we gonna get him out of here?"

"Maybe we don't?" The wheels in Honeybear's mind begin to turn, grinding slowly, gunked up with all the filth he can't stop thinking about. "Hear me out," Honeybear goes to the built-in, hollow wardrobe. "What if we make it look like he hung himself from this? Like he was doing it to get off?"

Babydoll squints like Honeybear just said the dumbest thing she's ever heard. "What? Like, how does that explain the neck wound or the burns? Not to mention the massive dent in his head!?"

"I got it!" Honeybear snaps his fingers. "We stick the curlers in his hand," he mines like he's hanging by the neck, holding the curling iron, "then oopsie-daisy, the rope broke and," Honeybear pretends to fall, "doof," smacking his head on the iron.

"That's... just stupid enough to work, but hurry, we need to make it look like it happened after we left."

"Okay, help me get him free," Honeybear kneels by the tipped chair and works at the binds, while Babydoll gets her handcuff keys from a fluffy pink purse and unlocks the ones around Clint's wrists.

"You got him?" Babydoll asks as Honeybear puts his arms under Clint's.

"I think… Jesus he's heavy!" Honeybear groans as he drags Clint's body up off the floor. "Ew-ew! We're touching swords!"

"Well, that's your fault for not wearing pants, you weirdo!"

The first flaw in Honeybear's plan rears its head. Clint's almost a foot taller than Honeybear, meaning he has to drag the corpse across the room with his feet trailing on the floor. This leads Babydoll to observe, "This is never gonna work. He's taller than the wardrobe."

"Huh?" Honeybear's foot slips, he stumbles backward and lands on the bed, hard on his ass, while

Clint's body flops face down on his lap.

Babydoll giggles. "Oh, Honeybear, you never said you wanted some extra dick too."

"Not funny!" Honeybear shudders. His eyes nearly pop out. "Get him off, get him off!"

"I mean, I already-"

"I mean it! He's drooling on my dick," Honeybear shudders, "I've got dead guy spit on my-Oh God no!" He goes rigid like a current's being fired through his body. "His tongue just fell on my balls. Help."

"Oh," Babydoll bites her lip and rubs a hand down her stomach, "that's hot."

"Not. Funny. Help."

"Hey, if he licks balls half as good as he does pussy you're in for a treat, Honeybear."

"Again, and I repeat, not funny!"

Babydoll thinks it is, though. Right up until the door opens.

Twenty-Four Seconds Earlier...

PING!

"Okay, I've changed my mind; we shouldn't do

this," Alana drags her feet as Bret hurries along the corridor.

"Stop being such a wuss," Bret's buzzing with excitement, brandishing his keycard up high like it's a set of marching orders.

"I really don't know if I wanna see, and he's gonna think I'm stalking him!"

"Girl, that's 'cause you are and," Bret swipes his card, "boop!"

"Bret!"

"In we go," Bret takes a deep breath and declares loudly, "Housekeeping!" as he pushes the door open to reveal the following tableau, frozen in embarrassed horror:

A nude man, on his knees, head on the lap of another man – this one with a face like he's just about to nut or, perhaps, keel over, it's hard to tell. In the middle of the room, body facing the men but head twisted to the door, an adorable Asian girl with cute as hell rainbow-colored hair in nothing but her underwear.

"Oh my god! I'm so sorry!" Bret closes the door, slowly enough to enjoy the scene, but quick enough to not make it obvious. Behind him, Alana stares, one eye-popping with a raised brow in utter stunned awe.

As soon as Bret closes the door, putting his back up against it, he breathes again, biting down on the urge to laugh.

"Wow," Alana finally says. "Guess that's that."

Bret fans himself, almost trembling with frenetic energy. Alana's seen this before; she calls it a *Brettsplosion* – when he gets so excited, he looks like a shook-up bottle of coke ready to pop.

"Calm yourself, and say it," she asks, knowing he's desperate to say but needs to calm down first.

"I know who she is!" Bret blurts out and takes off towards the elevator. He smashes the button over and over, fidgeting on the spot.

"Who!?" Alana calls after and makes it to the elevator as it pings open.

Bret doesn't answer; he jumps in before the doors are fully open and hits the button for the basement, swiping his keycard to authorize it.

"Bret! Spill!"

"I'll show you," the elevator doors close and moments later, his locker opens, Bret reaching in with that grin still on his face.

"Look!" He holds up a paperback copy of *Princess Bubblegum and The Slumber Party War*. The cover shows an anime girl from behind, hair in two different colored bunches, a flowing kaleidoscope cloak, and a candy-cane sword by her side facing down an approaching, shadowy arm of red-eyed creatures.

"Um, so you're still reading kids' books, okay"…"

Bret boops her on the head with it. He turns it around to show the back cover and points to the aut'or's photo – a smiling Asian woman with distinctive rainbow-colored hair.

"Oh my god!" Alana's jaw drops. "No way!"

"Yes, way!" Bret bounces on the spot. "That's Princess Bubblegum herself up there having a threeway!"

"That's, just… wow."

"I know! Do you think she'll sign my book!?"

"Do you think–"

"No," Babydoll interrupts, "they'd just think he was sucking you off, right?"

"No, do you think you can get him off me now!"

"Aw, but Honeybear, you look so hot with another guy on your dick," Babydoll teases, biting her finger and playing with her foot.

"Not cool."

"Hey, I do all the kinky stuff you ask for," she pouts, "I think it's only fair you put on a show for me?"

"If that were the case, Babydoll, love of my life, I'd fuck a dude while you're home doing the fucking dishes! Not in front of you!"

"Okay," Babydoll motions to the door, "I could go and give you two some time?"

"Time is something we do not have, light of my life. Please?"

"Urgh," Babydoll kicks air, "fine." As she comes over, she has a wicked thought. "Hey, what if this was like the start of a zombie movie? And he came back to life," she bites, clacking her teeth, "and chomped your dick right off?"

"So not cool!"

Babydoll grabs Clint by the shoulders and the back of his head. She pulls him back, then thrusts his head forward, growling, "num-num-num!"

Honeybear screams, crossing his arms over his chest as he shrivels in fear.

Clint's body slides to the floor as Babydoll doubles over, laughing her tiny ass off. "Oh God, your face!"

"Not — and I can't stress this enough— cool!"

Babydoll keeps laughing so hard she can't stay on her feet, and she drops to the floor, wiping tears of joy from her eyes.

Honeybear wipes the dead guy's spit from his crotch with the bedsheet. "I'm gonna need like fifty showers after that."

"Aw, but Honeybear, don't you want me to taste another man on your dick?"

"Okay, gross," he thinks about for a second, "but kinda hot, not gonna lie."

Babydoll gives him that *I'm just a naughty kitty* lip bite, and then her eyes fall to Clint's dead, naked body.

"It's kinda weird," she says. "Like, I thought I fucked a dead guy. I mean, not like that was on my Fuck It list or anything, but still..."

"Yeah, I think I get it," Honeybear kneels behind her, wrapping his Babydoll in his arms. He rests his head on her shoulder and kisses her cheek. "Mentally, you've already crossed that line, but you haven't really done it."

"It kinda feels like dreaming about doing something really wild, and then waking up, feeling sad it didn't actually happen."

"I know," he hugs her tighter, and Babydoll holds onto his forearm. "Usually, when you have one of those kinky dreams, we can make it happen later."

"Yeah..."

"You wanna fuck him, don't you?"

"Kinda... is that wrong?"

"It's pretty fucked, Babydoll, not gonna lie."

"Yeah. What's wrong with me?"

"I dunno," he kisses her again, "but fuck it, I love it."

"You're the best," Babydoll lifts his hand to her mouth, kissing it.

"I'll get our stuff while you—"

"No," Babydoll slides his hand inside her bra. "I want you both inside me. Together." She arches her back, twisting her neck and lips towards him. "I want us to do it together," she whispers and bites his ear.

Honeybear grunts, "Shit, you got me hard," he nods to the corpse, "better work on him."

Babydoll leans over and starts working Clint's cock. She's rough, doesn't have to be considerate, and she jerks it so fast, so hard, she's liable to rip the foreskin free.

Honeybear leans back, stroking his own cock as he watches Babydoll's bent-over ass wiggle. He hooks her panties with his other hand, pulling them down enough to expose her pussy. Licking his fingers, Honeybear slides two inside her. They glide in with no resistance, she's already soaking wet. She still hasn't showered, there hasn't been time, and for that he's grateful. There's nothing quite like the scent of his Babydoll's pussy after it's spent the night fermenting with another man's juices.

Babydoll starts rocking on his fingers, pushing herself down them as she moans, making it easy for Honeybear to tickle her asshole with his thumb. She likes that too and goes even harder, so Honeybear can stick it in her. She groans to the beat of wet slapping, feeling Honeybear's cock tapping off her cheeks as he works it – spittles of pre-cum leaving wet streaks, like a signature.

Then, suddenly, Babydoll stops. "It's not working."

"Huh?" Honeybear says and carefully pops his thumb out of his girlfriend's asshole, the other two fingers in her pussy following effortlessly.

"He's not getting hard," Babydoll complains, slapping Clint's limp, dead dick.

"Shit, look, Babydoll, no way you can take that personally."

She pouts, absolutely taking it personally.

"Maybe dead, like actual dead-dead, guys can't get hard, you know?"

"Or he doesn't think I'm hot," Babydoll sighs.

"Hey!" Honeybear spins her around, "Listen, you're the hottest little bubblegum slut™ in the whole fucking world, you hear me?"

She continues to sulk.

"You're so fucking cute but just filthy, filthy-minded, like a pixie bitch in five-inch heels and nothing but panties that say *Return to My Boyfriend Full*. Babydoll, I am forever in awe of your stunning depravity."

There's a flicker of a smile on her lips, his words cracking through.

"I don't wanna watch you fuck so much just because I'm just some sick pervert-"

"You are, and I love that about you," she strokes his cheek.

"I wanna watch you fuck because you're the hottest thing on the planet, and it's a fucking crime to keep you to myself. To miss out on that show. You're my favorite pornstar, my best friend, and the woman I love more than life itself."

"Honeybear!" Babydoll throws herself into his arms and hugs her head right to his chest. "I love you too, like crazy, stupid love. You know it's only fun doing all this kinky shit because I know you love it? Right? I might fuck other guys, but I'm your *Bubblegum Slut*, and yours alone. I'd be just as happy if I only ever fucked you for the rest of my life."

"I know, Babydoll," he strokes her hair. "And that's why I trust you to do whatever fucked up, kinky thing comes into that sexy mind of yours."

"Anything?"

"Absolutely. No limits. You want it, you got it."

"Would you fuck him while I watch?"

"Huh?"

"Is it weird? I mean, you always get off on me fucking other guys, but sometimes I worry. Like, I've probably fucked more than a hundred different guys—"

"Probably?"

"And you only ever fuck me. Now and then, I kinda wish you would fuck someone else," Babydoll looks to the side sheepishly. "I know you say I shouldn't, but I feel guilty sometimes."

"Babydoll, you know I don't want to fuck anyone else."

"But…"

"I know you'd let me. I know you'd be happy with me doing it," Honeybear shrugs, "but I like it this way. I dunno, it just works, right?"

"Yeah," Babydoll nods; for the second time in so many minutes, this remarkable man has reminded her of just why she loves him so much. "Sometimes, though, I like to think about maybe watching you fuck a guy? Like if you don't wanna bang another girl, okay, but maybe?"

Honeybear recalls something that suddenly makes a lot of sense. "Is this why you shove your dildo in my mouth after you get yourself off with it?"

"Uh-huh," she shrugs. "That's a real Manuel Ferrara dildo, so it's kinda like you're licking my lady juice from his actual cock." Her eyes roll back, "that gets me so wet, look," she reaches into her panties and pulls out a shiny, sticky fingers.

Honeybear's lips part instinctively as the scent of her reaches him, and Babydoll puts her fingers in his mouth.

"I have this fantasy," Babydoll slides her fingers deeper. "You getting the guy ready to fuck me, sucking him till he's hard," she groans, shoving her fingers all the way in, "licking me till I'm ready for his cock."

Honeybear cleans her fingers, thoroughly, and her fantasy gives rise to conflicting sensations — that addictive combination of repulsion and temptation — not to mention his dick. He's never wanted to suck another guy off before, or even given it any real thought, but hearing his Babydoll put it in that context makes his dick so hard it bounces like a puppy pulling on the lead, eager to go for a run.

When she takes her fingers back, Honeybear looks deep into her eyes. "Stand up," he orders, and she complies. "Take your panties off." She does that, too, stepping out of them, never breaking eye contact.

"Now go sit on his face," Honeybear nods to Clint's corpse.

Babydoll pads across the floor and steps over the body. She lowers herself onto Clint's twisted face, turning his head so his nose rubs against her pussy.

"What are you doing?" Babydoll asks, slowly sliding herself up along Clint's face.

Honeybear spits on his hand, then uses it to wet his dick. "Giving you what you need, Babydoll," he says and pushes his way between Clint's legs, spreading them with his hips. The familiar maneuver takes on a thrilling and new frisson as he feels entirely different skin against his. Clint's legs are hairless, he's a swimmer after all, but the weight and muscle tone are something new.

Babydoll melts as she watches Honeybear guide his cock towards Clint's body, falling forward hard onto his chest.

"Wait," she gasps, "wait-wait." Biting her lip, she asks, "play with his cock first?"

"Is that what Babydoll needs?"

"Uh-huh."

Honeybear grabs Clint's cock without further hesitation. It's the first time he's held another man's dick, never mind a dead one, and it doesn't feel half as strange as he thought it would. It's cold and limp, but that's not what matters. No, it's that look Babydoll's giving him that tells him everything. How much she wants this. She grinds so hard against the dead guy's face that if she weren't so wet, she'd start a fire.

"Suck him," Babydoll begs, "please?"

Honeybear leans over and takes Clint's cock in his mouth. The coldness feels off, vaguely like eating damp sushi, and he finds himself wishing it would get full and hard.

"Can you taste me on him?" Babydoll groans as she rides. "Huh, Honeybear? Can you taste my cum on his cock?"

That nearly makes him shoot his load all over the dead guy's legs, so Honeybear pops the dick out of his mouth and stops jerking himself.

"I want you to clean all my cum from his cock," Babydoll orders. "Pull back his skin."

Honeybear does as she asks, exposing the head of Clint's cock. He never really noticed on the video or last night, but it's round and thick, like a microphone.

"Lick all my cum from it," Babydoll rides even harder, and if Clint's neck was broken before, that would probably do it. Honeybear holds Clint's dick at an angle so Babydoll can see him run his tongue up, around the head, and then all the way to the tip, parting it, flicking his tongue, while never breaking eye contact.

"Oh God," Babydoll's eyes turn white, and she holds back. "Let me get you ready."

She crawls across the corpse and takes her Honeybear's dick in her mouth, slobbering over it till he's slick with drool. Her other hand goes to her pussy, slathering it with her wetness. Once she's done, she smears her juices all over Honeybear's cock and spits on it, drooling as she lubricates him.

"Fuck him now," Babydoll orders.

Honeybear drops the dead guy's dick, moves in, and guides his cock below Clint's balls. There's resistance, so he has to really shove it, but it's not like Clint's going to complain. Once it's in, Honeybear goes for it, thrusting away at full-speed with no warm-up. Not because time is of the essence, but because he's so turned on he just has to. He feels Clint's ass try to push him out, so Honeybear moves in closer, forcing Clint to take even more of his dick.

"Oh, God… Yeah, fuck him!" Babydoll screams.

"Fucking ride his face!" Honeybear roars.

They both go hard, fast, in perfect sync, leaning in till their heads meet. Both grasp the back of the other's head, pulling hair and breathing heavily onto one another. Both love that they're sharing this moment, crossing another threshold together, becoming one as they fuck a dead guy. This is definitely a *hashtag couplegoals*.

"I'm gonna cum," Honeybear gasps.

"Wait for me," Babydoll sighs.

"Okay," Honeybear holds back, but it's tough. Babydoll kisses him passionately, and when their lips part, he asks, "you ready?"

"Ready," she whines, and they kiss again, almost chewing each other's faces as they cum. Honeybear empties himself inside Clint, dick pumping over and over as he fills the dead guy's ass with hot, warm cum and Babydoll gushes all over his face, grinding it into the floor as she squirts.

They collapse together, sweaty, smiling, using Clint's chest as a pillow.

"That was the hottest," Babydoll says through gasping giggles.

"Yeah," Honeybear signs, "woo, God Damn."

They turn, looking at one another, basking in that post-orgasm glow.

"I love you, Babydoll."

"I love you, Honeybear."

And they lie there for a while, chests heaving in tandem, slowly coming down, and just as they're both ready to slip into a post-fuck doze, their eyes shoot wide open. They turn to each other once more and, together, they panic –"What time is it!?"

Scrambling for their phones, Honeybear finds his first and lights it up. "Shit, it's just gone eleven."

"What time is check out?" Babydoll flaps her hands as she paces back and forth, wrought with worry.

"Half-past," Honeybear gulps, "we got thirty minutes to figure out what we're gonna do with him."

"Shit," Babydoll chews on her finger nervously. "Shit-shit."

"Just pack your stuff up; I'll think of something," Honeybear says, rubbing the back of his head. He has no fucking clue what he's gonna do, but getting their shit together is at least a step in the right direction. He watches as Babydoll wheels her case out, tipping the thing over and unzipping it. Maybe it's the way she kneels next to it, clearly small enough to fit...

"Babydoll, I have an idea," Honeybear's suddenly alive with an exuberance of confidence. "We take him with us." He drops down next to the case. "Wheel him right out the door."

"But what about my makeup and stuff?" Babydoll clutches some palettes to her chest.

"Fit what you can in my backpack. Ditch some of you have to."

Babydoll gasps like he just asked her to abandon her childhood dog. "Not my Kat Von D limited-edition eye shadow palette!"

"Okay, not that one, but–"

"No! That's my MAC foundation set."

Honeybear stares deadpan. His finger lifts, pointing to another plastic case.

"But, but that's my Urban Decay."

"All right! Fine, throw any of my shit away if you gotta, just empty this case and shove it all in my bag."

The two of them quickly empty Babydoll's suitcase; there's not as much in it as it looked – just that

Babydoll can't pack for shit. While she tries to Tetris everything into Honeybear's small, vintage backpack, he squats by Clint's corpse.

"Hey man, so I guess I should say thanks for a hell of a time. Sorry you died and all, but hey, what guy doesn't want to die fucking some insanely hot girl?"

"Aw, Honeybear!"

"You're my Queen, Baby," he says without looking back and then turns to the corpse. "Anyhoo, we gotta get you in there. You'd understand, right? So, um," he takes Clint's flaccid hand, "put it there, buddy," and shakes it.

"Okay, how we gonna do this," Babydoll and Honeybear stand over the empty case, trying to picture it.

"How 'bout," Honeybear hops in the case, sitting down with his knees slightly bent to fit, and leans over till he touches his feet.

"I dunno," Babydoll plays with her mouth, "he's a lot taller; I don't think he'll fit."

"Shit, yeah, you're right. Oh, what about fetal?" Honeybear curls up on his side, pulling his knees to his chest, and it looks like there's plenty of room.

"Maybe, but his shoulders are too wide to fit that way."

"Oh, come on," Honeybear leans out of the case, shouting at Clint's body. "Seriously, man, why you gotta be so fucking perfect."

"Honeybear," Babydoll takes his face in her hands,

"don't say that. I mean, sure, he's, was, hot as fuck, but he's not you," she kisses him "to me, you're perfect."

"Aw," Honeybear tears up, "and you're perfect for me." He takes one of her hands and kisses it. "I think this can work; we'll just sit on the case till it shuts. Not like it matters if we break anything else, right?"

"Good point," she agrees.

Together they drag the corpse to the case, lifting him over the edge and placing him side down. Babydoll tucks his head in while Honeybear pushes Clint's knees till he's curled up inside the case. She goes to close it over and Honeybear stops her.

"Think you're gonna need a new one of these," he says, holding up the dirty, bloody, and sticky curling iron. Babydoll sighs and nods, as he throws it in the case.

"That was a limited-"

"I know, Babydoll," he puts his arm around her, "I know."

They drop the lid, and there's a good couple of inches gap. Lining up, side by side, facing away from the case, they nod to signal they're ready and, as one, drop their butts down.

The case closes tight, with a sickening crunch and rip. Even though Clint's already dead, it still makes them wince. They reach for the zip and begin closing it up.

"Oh, shit," Babydoll curses, "we broke the lock."

"So, as long as it's shut?"

"I guess," Babydoll sighs. "I really loved this case, you know."

"I know, come on, let's get some clothes on and get the fuck out of here."

"Okay," Babydoll says, and as she pulls yesterday's clothes on quickly, and Honeybear hops into his jeans, neither of them notices the zip on the case slowly, incrementally, moving.

Walk of Shame

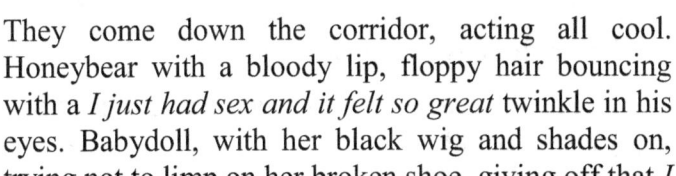

They come down the corridor, acting all cool. Honeybear with a bloody lip, floppy hair bouncing with a *I just had sex and it felt so great* twinkle in his eyes. Babydoll, with her black wig and shades on, trying not to limp on her broken shoe, giving off that *I feel Daddy as fuck attitude.*

Honeybear swipes their card at the elevator, and they wait.

PING!

It arrives, opens, and it's, thankfully, empty. Babydoll wheels the case in with them, and Honeybear hits the button for the lobby. The door closes, and they both feel like they can breathe again.

"Just hand the keycard over," Babydoll explains. "I'll go straight for the door."

Honeybear nods.

"We're just two totally normal guests checking out," Babydoll says. "Just say good morning, nod, act like nothing's up."

"Yeah," Honeybear nods. "Except for my…"

"Are you serious!?"

"I like you in those shades!" Honeybear fixes his pants. "Every time you put them on, I remember that photo Ally took of you."

"In Cancun?"

"Yeah."

"On the nude beach?"

"Oh, yeah."

"With those two guys we–"

"I know what you did. Disgusting behavior," Honeybear coughs.

"You fucking love it," she laughs. "Besides, you know the rules. Anything goes on a girl's trip."

PING!

The elevator reaches the top floor, the door opens, and Honeybear gulps as Alana stands on the other side. She hesitates for a moment and steps inside.

"Morning," she says, tucking her hair behind her ear, unable to bring herself to look at either of them. She turns her back to them, "Going down?"

"What, like for murder?" Honeybear laughs too hard.

"No…" Alana squints. "The lobby?"

Honeybear nods, Babydoll shoots him an *I can not*

fucking believe you stare. He mimes he's sorry.

An awkward silence follows, broken only by the steady, slow rip of a zip coming undone. Babydoll's eyes follow the sound to her case, and it's a good thing her pitch-black Ray-Bans hide her eyes cause the fear in them would be unmistakable.

"Listen," Alana cringes, "I'm sorry for this morning."

Babydoll slaps Honeybear's arm and draws his attention to the case as the zip pops and Clint's hand flops out.

"Walking in on you guys," Alana continues. "We thought the room was ready for tossing. No, that's a lie. I saw on the camera…it doesn't matter. I deleted the footage. Can we just forget this happened?"

"Sure," Babydoll chirps as she thrashes silently, arms flailing as she tries to tell Honeybear to keep Alana busy.

"And I'm really sorry for last night," Alana bites down. She begins to turn, and Honeybear, understanding his Babydoll's instructions on some unspoken level, darts around to Alana's front.

"Hey, it's all good," he says, leaning against the wall, arm up behind his head, rubbing his neck. "No harm done."

Babydoll tries to force the hand back in, only for the zip to pop more, and Clint's foot sticks out.

"No, I was out of line." Alana looks at her shoes. "I shouldn't have hit on you."

Babydoll's head jerks up like a greedy kitty hearing the rustling of a treat bag. Honeybear tries to wave it off, then flips back to cool and poised as Alana looks up.

"I'm sorry," she says again.

"Honestly," Honeybear waves a hand, "no harm done."

Clint's other arm plunks out, and Babydoll makes angry little fists in frustration.

"It's just, I'm sorry, but you're like ridiculously cute," Alana says and begins to turn around. "I didn't mean, I know–"

"Hey!" Honeybear yells. Alana jerks back to face him. "You think?"

"Yeah," Alana laughs, "even more 'cause you don't act like you know it. Oh my god, I'm so sorry, right in front of your..."

Alana begins to turn again.

Babydoll mouths two words, *kiss*, and *her*. She's about to add *now* and *bitch* when Honeybear does what he's told. Just as Alana's eyes approach the dead guy's arm sticking out of Babydoll's suitcase, Honeybear puts a hand on her cheek, turns her face to him, and leans in for the kiss.

Their lips touch and Alana's whole body goes rigid for just a second, and then her hands are reaching for Honeybear's hoodie - pulling herself closer to him as their tongues meet. She moans and then goes at Honeybear like she's cleaning a whisk with her mouth.

Babydoll tilts her shades down to watch. The sight of another woman pinning her man to the wall sends a shock wave of lust through her body. It's such a turn-on that she completely forgets about the dead guy's arm sticking out the suitcase.

Honeybear, eyes wide, uses them to pull Babydoll's attention back to the task at hand. She shakes off the horny and shoves the hand back in violently. The case clatters off the wall, drawing Alana's attention, but just as she's about to break the kiss, Honeybear covers by slapping the wall behind him, moaning dramatically.

PING!

The elevator comes to a stop.

ZIP!

Babydoll closes the case and celebrates with a silent little fist pump.

Honeybear pulls out of the kiss, and Alana stumbles back, bracing herself against the wall. Her chest heaves, eyes wide in stunned disbelief at what just happened.

"Don't sweat it," Honeybear throws her a thumbs up and hops out the elevator. Babydoll follows though she pauses to give Alana a wink before pushing her shades back up. She's so flustered she stays pinned to the wall as the doors close on her.

"Awesome room, five stars," Honeybear says as he tosses the keycards to one of the black shirts by the podium. Babydoll's already heading towards the door, and he hurries to catch up.

"You have to tell me all about that girl hitting on you." Babydoll smirks.

"No, I don't," Honeybear tries to give her the attitude, and it just doesn't work. All it takes is a glance to make him crack. "Okay, she was all drunk at the bar last night and came onto me. Said you were probably getting deep-dicked–"

Babydoll snorts. "It's like she knows me or something."

"And I shouldn't feel bad about getting a little something-something 'cause of that."

"She's not wrong, Honeybear. I mean, she's hot."

"Yeah?"

"Oh, yeah. I'd hit that for sure," Babydoll giggles.

"Okay, we're gonna have to revisit that idea when we're clear of this mess."

"Sure," Babydoll grins, "still doesn't mean I'm gonna let you watch."

Honeybear grumbles, and before he can say

anything else, a yell from behind makes him flinch.

"Hey!"

They both look over their shoulders to see one of the black-shirted hotel staff waving at them.

"STOP!"

Babydoll and Honeybear's eyes meet. "Shit," they say in unison and then look ahead. Picking up the pace, Babydoll struggles with only one heel on her shoes; they go as fast as possible while still trying to look casual.

"Wait up!" The black shirt calls and both of them can hear the squeak of his sneakers on the floor as he sprints towards them. The door's just there; they can make it.

They're right at the door, and then the black shirt whips past, blocking the way. He doubles over, beads of sweat all over his head.

Honeybear and Babydoll tense up.

"Sorry," the black shirt gasps, "I know," he heaves, "I'm being weird, but this is you, right?" Black shirt holds up a paperback copy of Princess Bubblegum and The Slumber Party War, showing them the back cover with Babydoll's photo. "Right?"

She glances at Honeybear, and he shrugs. They've been made. What can they do now?

"Yeah," Babydoll drags out each syllable.

"Could you sign it, please?" Black shirt produces a pen from his pocket and thrusts that with the book towards Babydoll. "Please?"

"Of course," Babydoll takes both and opens to the front page. "Who should I–"

"Bret, please," he smiles, "I'm such a fan you have no idea!" As Babydoll scrawls her name, he chances his luck. "So, could you tell me if Himiko and Ren are gonna-"

"Uh-uh," Babydoll pauses, "spoilers."

"Please! I can't… my heart can't take it. Like everyone keeps thinking they don't make sense, and she's too mean to him, but I just know that's her love language. They just love each other on some insanely deep level that outsiders can't see. They just have to get together! Please?"

"Sorry," she finishes up and hands the book back to him. "Nice meeting you!" She puts on the cute and waves as she and Honeybear head out through the door, a dead guy hidden safely inside their suitcase.

Bret holds the book to his chest, and only when they're gone from sight does he open it and read the inscription. He gasps in delight, and his heart flutters at the love heart with the names Himiko and Ren inside it.

"Dearly beloved, we are gathered here today to say farewell to Clint, though he leaves this world we shall always remember–"

"Not the time," Babydoll moans.

They're on a bridge, somewhere on the edge of the city, traffic is light, and the river below gargles like Babydoll with a mouthful of cum. That comparison earned Honeybear a slap as they got out of their car.

The suitcase with Clint's body rests on the ground between them.

"Fine," Honeybear looks around, checking no cars are coming.

"Wait," Babydoll opens the zip a little. "We want water to get in, so it sinks, and fish can get to him."

Honeybear stares at her, a little scared.

"What? I have to think about these things."

"For your books. Right?"

Babydoll pats the suitcase.

"Right!?"

"All good. Quickly, before we get caught."

Keenly aware she didn't answer his questions, Honeybear reckons it's best to just do as she says. Together they lift the case, slide it over the railing, and push it over the edge with a nod.

It splashes down below, and Honeybear puts his arm around Babydoll. They watch as the current takes the suitcase, as it bobs in and out of view, as it slips away from sight, carried away towards the ocean.

"It's kinda like a Viking funeral," Honeybear nods.

"Clint was a swimmer, a man of the waves, and now the waves take him."

"That's kinda nice," Babydoll squeezes into him. "I'm gonna steal that for the new book."

They stand together in comfortable silence as it sinks in the night and all the complications that arose from it are finally over.

"So, that happened..." Honeybear says through his busted lip.

"Yup," Babydoll says, all her weight on the shoe not missing a heel.

Slowly, they turn to look one another in the eye. He sighs, she gulps, and together they say, "I fucking love you," and kiss.

S e v e r a l   M o n t h s   L a t e r . . .

———————|———————

Honeybear looks at his phone, giddy with excitement.

He opens his camera app, points it down, and snaps a photo of an open box stuffed with thin, glossy books. Author copies of a children's storybook called Honeybear and Babydoll's Big City Adventure — a cute, colorful anime ragdoll and a doting teddy bear following on her heels as she runs through a neon city.

He adds the caption: *look what came in* and sends it.

"Okay, back to work," he says to himself and heads to the kitchen when a pile of dishes awaits him. On the way, he passes the remnants of a birthday celebration, a large piece of custom art waiting to be put on the wall rests against the sofa. It shows a superhero gangbang, with numerous half-naked capes giving it to and waiting for their turn with a very familiar looking rainbow-haired masked heroine. A discarded strap-on lies on the floor near it, perhaps explaining the odd limp in Honeybear's step.

He puts his phone on the kitchen counter and fills the sink, getting on with the task. Just as he's cleaning a glass, his phone buzzes and he looks at the screen.

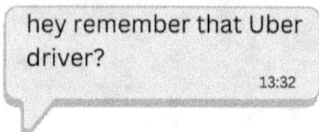

hey remember that Uber
driver?

13:32

Seconds pass.

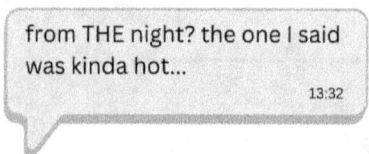

from THE night? the one I said
was kinda hot...

13:32

The glass clatters into the sink, and Honeybear feels his dick get hard just from that text.

A notification says he's received a photo, but he can't see it on the lock-screen.

"Shit," Honeybear curses and can't find a towel to dry his hands with, so he grabs the phone with soapy fingers. He can't get the fingerprint lock to work, so he waits, impatiently, for facial recognition, and then, finally, he opens the image.

It's a selfie, shot from a high angle. Babydoll's arm is in the shot, holding the phone. Behind her, there's a naked man, ball-gagged and tied to a chair. It looks like they're in a garage or somewhere industrial. Babydoll's got her hair scraped back, a black latex bra on, and bites the tip of her finger.

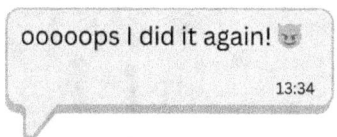

"Oh, God Damn!" Honeybear cheers.

The three dots appear on the screen; Babydoll's typing, but he's too excited, and the phone slips.

"No!"

It plops into the sink.

"Ah, shit!"

Credits

I wrote this story because somebody called my writing wholesome. Imagine an angry raccoon screaming at his laptop "I'll show how fucking wholesome I am!" My one guiding principle was to always make everything one step more perverse than I initially imagined. In the end though my tendency towards tenderness sort of bled through. I don't know if you can call a story like this cute, but I'd like to think I got close.

It's also really hard to research this kink without so much noise and misunderstandings and I'm not sure those who helped want their names out there, but thank you anyway. Soft White Underbelly's YouTube Channel was also super helpful with understanding some of this.

Big thanks to Alana K. Drex and Bret Laurie for reading early drafts, their feedback and being part of this fucked up story. Dawn Shea from D&T Publishing for taking Babydoll on and, of course, Casey, my partner who encouraged me to try writing something more smutty. In many ways, this is all her fault. If you think about it.

ABOUT THE AUTHOR

———————|———————

Christopher Robertson writes cinematic pulp fiction that's often described as both wholesome and gruesome, sometimes in the same sentence. He won both the Gold award for Best Novel and Silver for Best Audiobook at the 2023 Godless 666 Awards.

terrorscopestudios@gmail.com

Instagram: @kit_romero

TikTok: @terrorscopestudios

ABOUT THE PUBLISHER/EDITOR

Dawn Shea is an author and half of the publishing team over at D&T Publishing. She lives with her family in Mississippi. Always an avid horror lover, she has moved forward with her dreams of writing and publishing those things she loves so much.

Follow her author page on Amazon for all publications she is featured in.

Follow D&T Publishing at their website, **www.dandtpublishing.com**, or search for their Facebook Group

Or email here: dandtpublishing20@gmail.com

Babydoll by Christopher Robertson

Edited by Tasha Schiedel

Cover by Christopher Robertson

Formatting by Ash Ericmore